For Dad,
Thanks for showing me all of the scary movies as
a kid.

While she sleeps, time breaks,
when she wakes, time ends.

SHE WHO SLEEPS BENEATH THE TREES

KRISTOPHER JEROME

Paperback ISBN: 978-1-951138-21-9

ALSO FROM DARK TIDINGS PRESS

THE GODS AND MEN CYCLE

By Kristopher Jerome

The Broken Pact Trilogy:

- Wrath of the Fallen
- Cries of the Forsaken
- Tears of the Godless

The Nightbreaker

White Wings from Grey Ash

Before the Breaking:

- A Bandit's Balance
- A Voice from the Darkness
- In the Shadow of Light
- The Sons of Lighthammer
- The Bard's Demons
- Disciples of the First Cycle
- Ten of Seatown
- The Last Gift of Kane Darksend
- The Grey God's Edict
- The Blood-Soaked Sacrament

BACKWOODS GRINDHOUSE

By Kristopher Jerome

She Who Sleeps Beneath the Trees

SHE WHO SLEEPS
BENEATH THE TREES

1

It was a bad night to have bald tires—even in an all-wheel drive. The rain that pelted Trey's windshield was starting to become sleet, as the autumn storm tore through the Columbia Gorge. The road here was bumpy and flooding, causing his seatbelt to cut into his newly flabby midsection. *The joys of turning 30.* To compound his frustration, he had no idea where he was going.

"Come on, you piece of shit," he said, slapping his dash like it was the car's fault the satellites couldn't find him in the woods. "I just want to see how close I am!"

Just the one road, the guy in Cascade Locks, a town back, had said. *Follow it until you get there, though most people don't want to.* Trey thought the creepy gas station attendant would have made for a good Stephen King character had he been older. Instead, he was just some pock-marked kid making some money after school to buy weed. The only reason Trey even took the time to ask for directions while he was filling up was because he knew that his phone's GPS would likely be unreliable somewhere this...remote.

After a few more minutes of being able to see nothing but trees behind a veil of rain and ice, he decided to pull over and see if he could wait out the worst of it. Little good it would do his book to flip his car or run into some drunk in the dark. A peal of thunder made him jump in his seat just as he drifted onto what muddy patch constituted the shoulder of this "Highway" and turned off his engine.

Jackson Road, or the Jackson Highway, it was called. The one winding trail from Cascade Locks to the "town" of Jackson Point. Trey liked to put quotes around the word "town" when he thought of the place because it was actually an unincorporated community that for some reason still pretended to be the real deal. They had their own mayor, city council, and a small police force, from what he found in his research. But for whatever reason, they had never officially incorporated to join the rest of Oregon in the 21st century.

"Fucking hillbilly shit," he grumped as he pulled out his laptop.

Flipping the screen up, he saw the battery light flashing in the corner. Only 3% left. Of course, he had forgotten to charge it when he was packing the night before. After slamming the screen back down, he fished around in his backpack for a small Moleskine notebook. Styling himself as a classical journalist, this had been one of his first purchases right out of college; though he had never written anything past the first page. The headlights finally cut out just as he put pen to paper.

October 14th-Monday.

I left Portland in the late after-noon, just as the shadows began to stretch and darken. I had driven I-84 a few times in the past, making the inevitable pilgrimage of every Oregonian to Multnomah Falls a few times in my college days. Never before, though, had I stopped in the small town of Cascade Locks. Scenic in its own right, the small community was not my destination, however, but the gateway to somewhere far darker.

He chewed on the end of his pen for a few moments, trying to decide whether the tone was too pompous. He thought it might work for the blog—even the podcast, if he made it more conversational—but did it work for the opening lines of a book?

Trey had never written longer copy than a newspaper article or a blog post. Hell, most of his writing since the 2020 lockdown had been scripts for his podcast *The Dead and the Undead*. This would be his first foray into the world of true-crime literature, and he didn't want to fuck it up.

Jackson Point was founded in

He scribbled that line out. No one would care about the history of the town, not until it mattered to the case, anyway. And at this point, Trey didn't know what would matter to the case. He didn't know shit except that there were at least five bodies—and no suspects. This sleepy little "town" was the site of a prolific serial killer, and until now, no one was reporting on it.

The tip that brought me here said that so far, five bodies had been found mangled around town. The details of the killings were being kept hush-hush by the local police department, but my source says that the rumor is that they were partially devoured. Was Jackson Point hiding the next Dahmer? I intended to find out.

Another peal of thunder interrupted him, this one followed by a flash of white that illuminated the treeline—and something else. A large, gangly shape seemed to have been standing in the road some twenty feet in front of his car. Trey felt his heart slam against his ribcage as he dropped his pen and reached for the ignition button. A second later, the engine roared to life, and his headlights cut a swath through the murk of the forest road. Nothing was there.

Trey slapped his forehead and muttered to himself, "Fucking Stephen King hillbilly shit."

He had grown up in the Willamette Valley before moving north to Portland. Having never been in a city with fewer than 50,000 people, Trey had a habit of looking down on country types. He didn't understand the allure of the wilderness, especially with Oregon weather.

Even though the road was clear, the hairs on the back of his neck were standing on end, and Trey decided that he would rather try continuing to his destination with bald tires in a storm than waiting for whatever Hills Have Eyes shit was out here. The podcaster flicked on his blinker and returned to the road, driving ahead much slower than he had previously. His eyes flitted back and forth with the wiper blades, scanning the trees for some sign of whatever it was that he had seen. *Most people don't want to.* How in the world had he let that stoner gas station attendant get under his skin so badly?

The road continued to wind and climb with the topography here. While Cascade Locks had sat low along the Columbia, Jackson Point was higher and nestled between two mountains whose names he couldn't remember. What this meant was that even though the two towns were barely 5 miles apart as the crow flies, this road, especially in this weather, would take the better part of an hour to traverse. And Trey had already been at it for 45 minutes or more.

Finally, the rain started to slow, and the thunder seemed to have moved farther to the west. This change in the weather gave Trey the confidence to pick up his speed and take the sloping turns with a little more daring. He doubted he would see another car tonight, and unless Sasquatch or whatever the hell he had imagined had been real, he wouldn't see much else either.

Around the next curve, the road seemed to straighten a bit, until the distant treeline swallowed it up. *For a logging community, there sure are a lot of trees left,* he thought. There was no further sign of Bigfoot, and by the time the road curved again, the rain was completely gone. Trey couldn't help but crack a smile as he thought about what this book and podcast special would mean for his career. If he had thought he was big-time before, he was gonna really make it now.

Suddenly, the road forked in front of him, one side curving out of sight and the other continuing on straight for a ways before he couldn't see it anymore. He slowed to a stop just between the two roads and took off his glasses to rub his eyes. *He said there was just the one road.* Realizing that he had no functioning map and he didn't want to get stuck driving forever in the backwoods, Trey decided to get out and see if there was any indicator which direction led to Jackson Point.

Both sides of the fork looked the same to him in the dark, which is to say, barely paved and full of waterlogged potholes. *Why couldn't there be a sign?* Then he saw it, lying half hidden by the ferns and bushes that were trying to take back the forest floor from the highway. Trey swallowed and looked around again, just to be certain that he wasn't about to see a cougar or something before stumbling off the road into the sickly wet underbrush. Once he got to the sign, he saw that it seemed to have been slammed into by a car and sheared from the ground. He swallowed again as he thought of his earlier desire to avoid drunks on the road. The sign read: *Private Drive Left. Jackson Point 10 miles right.*

"10 miles," he whispered. "No way. How long is this this fucking highway?"

Climbing back into his car, he swung to the right and continued on, much slower this time. By the time the sign reading: *Welcome to Jackson Point* jumped out of the trees to greet him, he was nearly asleep. Somehow, it was after midnight now, which meant it was the 15th. How that was possible, he had no idea, but he chalked it up to spending more time parked than he had first realized. Thankfully, his room at the Best Boarding House was available for him to check into at any hour, or so the owner had said in the email.

The trees finally opened up somewhat, and the sleepy little "town" greeted him. There were few streetlights, and not a single window shone amber in the darkness. He shivered in spite of himself. Portland was never this dark. It was unnerving.

Based on the directions he had been given, the boarding house was going to be up on the right of Main Street, some three blocks down. Not that he expected that he would have needed directions, even in the dark. Jackson Point probably only had five streets.

He crawled past the first stop sign, trying to take in the small buildings that stood out in the darkness around him. A small gas station with just two pumps was the first building he passed, followed by what looked like a burger stand and a warehouse or something. With nothing but the dim streetlights, it was hard to tell. The next block seemed to be the important one: he could make out a large building with golden letters that reflected the streetlights. It said Library. The building beside it had white columns in front—likely the city hall. On the other side was a small firehouse and an even smaller police station. He crossed one more stop sign—did this place even have traffic lights?—and found himself outside the Best Boarding House.

At first, when making his reservation, he had thought the name rather presumptuous until he had seen the email signed *Carol Best*. That meant the name wasn't just presumptuous, but was actually a bad pun on top of it. Even so, they didn't have any motels in town, so this was the best he would get. He parked in one of the numbered spots out front and grabbed his backpack and his duffel. Gathering himself with a deep breath, Trey walked up the steps to the Victorian-style house and knocked on the door, as instructed.

After a few minutes of shivering in the post-storm air, a frail old woman with rheumy eyes and oxygen tubes in her nose opened the door with a scowl.

"Do you have any idea what time it is?" she wheezed.

"I-I'm sorry," Trey mumbled. "In your email, you said I could check in at any time. I'm Trey." He extended a hand. "Treyton Savage."

"Do I look like I use email?" the woman asked.

"Uhh," Trey began.

"That would have been my grandson, Kevin. He handles the emails for me, but I told him no one checks in after 7!"

Trey swallowed. It was a small town, but it couldn't have been *that* small.

"Your grandson wouldn't happen to be Kevin Anderhoff, would he, Mrs. Best?"

The woman eyed Trey warily and sucked on her gums a good while before answering.

"Yes, that's him. How do you know his name?" she asked.

"He's actually the reason I'm here," Trey said. "Kevin reached out to me."

For a moment, he thought the old woman was going to faint. She clutched at the door with gnarled fingers and leaned against it. The sound of her oxygen tank hissed from behind her.

"That boy has gotten you into a heap of trouble, mister," she whispered, looking around at the street. "You'd best come inside. It's not safe to be out after dark. One is liable to feed the Rootmother as much as get where they are going at this hour."

With that, she turned and receded back into the twilight of the house. Trey clutched his bags tighter and followed. What a book this would be.

2

Its hands wrapped around the woman's throat, choking the life from her. She writhed in agony, her eyes rolling about in their sockets like a cow during slaughter. It leaned in closer to smell her fear. Then it opened its mouth and tore a ragged piece of her upper lip off. Warm blood filled its mouth, and the woman's muffled cries became gurgles.

Crimson ran down her black necktie and stained her white blouse. Soon her struggling ceased, and it tore open her blouse to begin feasting on softer flesh. It had cornered her far from the camp, where none would see. Here, her blood could feed the roots. Here, the Elder One could gain nourishment.

In the distance, the hollers of men felling a tree drifted to its ears. They were close. She could feel them, and through her, *it* could too. When it was done with the soft outer flesh of the breasts, it cracked her ribcage open to feast on the organs. This was its favorite part. This was the gift that the Elder One had given it.

When it had eaten its fill, it left the remains of the woman at the base of a great fir. The tendrils from below hungrily reached up for the scarlet succor it had provided. She would be pleased.

"Oi!" a voice called. "What are you doing there? Eh?"

It turned to see two men wearing dirty shirts and rough-spun pants held up by suspenders. They were caked in mud from their black boots to their shoulders. One of them held an axe and the other a rifle. Their looks of confusion quickly turned to revulsion.

"It's that *thing!*" The man with the axe shouted. "Sweet merciful Mary, it got another one. Shoot it, Lysander. *Shoot it!*"

It smelled the smoke of gunpowder. It felt the sting of lead. It heard the retort of the rifle. It ran.

The dreamer awoke in a cold sweat. The clock beside them read 7:32 AM, October 1st. They knew not where the dream came from, but they knew what it meant. There would be another body discovered today. This would be the second one in the last two weeks. Just as the first was precipitated by a dream, so was this one.

The others needed to know about this. Things were moving according to plan, even if the plan made the dreamer nervous. They rolled out of bed and made their way into the shower. Regardless of what would happen tonight, there was still work today, and they were nearly late.

3

It wasn't Trey's alarm that woke him up from his fitful sleep, but instead, the surprisingly warm rays of the sun beating on his face through the partially opened shutters. He sighed and sat up, wondering how late he had overslept. His phone said it was 9:30. Not terrible, but a later start than he wanted.

He pushed himself up and looked around the sparse boarding room. The style could definitely have been described as "old woman chic". The walls were papered in a peeling pink, and the bedspread had more frills and folds on it than he had ever seen before. In front of the solitary window sat a small wooden desk where he had placed his backpack the night before. On the far wall, the wooden-slatted doors to the closet hung ajar.

Trey decided that he could skip the shower today and got up to pick out some clothes from his duffel. The closet smelled like stale mothballs and the vague ammonia scent of cat piss. He wrinkled his nose in disgust and pulled out a fresh pair of jeans and a flannel. Once he was dressed, he gave himself a once-over in the mirror that was mounted on the back of the door. He stifled a small chuckle when he saw himself. The red and black flannel made him look as if he were trying to blend in with a city-dweller's idea of a logging town. His auburn hair, which had started to thin, was tousled from the night of restless sleep. He brushed it back into place with his hand and turned sideways to look at the new addition to his midsection. So much for getting in shape this year.

With a sigh, he shoved his notebook and some pens into his backpack and slung it over his shoulder. He would leave the laptop on the desk for now. There was no telling what the internet situation would be outside of the boarding house. As it was, his cell phone flickered from one to no bars constantly.

Quietly, Trey opened the dark cherry door and sidled out into the hallway. Something about the hardwood floors and wallpaper made him feel like he needed to tiptoe around the place, lest he wake up some sleeping elder. He crossed the narrow hallway and crept down the staircase to the entryway. From the kitchen, he could hear the faint buzz of a radio and smell coffee brewing.

His stomach grumbled, and he realized he hadn't had a bite to eat since the gas station jerky he had picked up back in Cascade Locks. The next hunger pang nearly sent him reeling, and he felt his legs buckle. It was almost as if he hadn't eaten in days rather than hours. Deciding that it wouldn't do him any good to pass out on his first day about town, he walked into the kitchen.

Mrs. Best sat at the table with a cup of coffee, thumbing through a well-worn bible. When she heard Trey, she motioned to the coffee pot and a pile of scones beside it. Her oxygen tank hissed quietly beside her.

"Thank you," Trey muttered, pouring coffee into a mug with a worn smiley face on it.

"There's a key hanging on the hook for you," Mrs. Best said. "That way, you don't have to wake me at odd hours of the night. I expect you to lock the door when you come home."

"Yes, sorry about that." Trey took a bite of the still-warm scone. "I was going to ask you where I could find your grandson, Kevin?"

"Where do you think a boy his age would be at this hour on a Friday? He's in school, of course."

Trey nearly choked on the scone. He washed the crumbs out of his airway with a gulp of coffee and then dumped the rest into the sink.

"School? I didn't realize he was—ah, I thought he was older."

Mrs. Best simply scowled at him and went back to flipping through her bible. She seemed to be looking for something specific but not finding it. Trey turned to walk back out of the kitchen when something else she said crawled to the forefront of his mind.

"Uh, what day did you say it was, Mrs. Best?" Trey asked. "I swore you said Friday?"

"I did," she muttered, not looking up. "Are you deaf?"

"No, it's just—ah—it's just that it's Tuesday, October 15th. I left Portland the night of the 14th and got here just past midnight."

This caused Mrs. Best to finally look up from her bible and give Trey a look that could have curdled milk. She eyed him for a few moments before wheezing in a good bit of oxygen.

"Yes, you did come in last night and woke me up just after midnight. But you didn't leave Portland on Monday unless you got yourself lost for three and a half days. It's the 18th."

As if that was that, she went back to thumbing through her bible with a renewed ferocity. Trey nodded dumbly and scurried out of the kitchen. He grabbed the key from the hook next to the door and slipped out into the morning.

❦

"The 18th," Trey mumbled to himself as he walked down the street. "That can't be right. That old woman is out of her mind."

Still, he was afraid to check the date on his phone. After leaving the house, he realized that he hadn't paid any attention to the date when he had glanced at the time in his room. There was no way that it was Friday. He hadn't lost nearly a week. There was no way.

Deciding that he would muster the courage to look at his phone after the morning air had a chance to clear his head, he continued heading south down Main Street to get a better idea of the layout of Jackson Point. Next to the Best Boarding House was a much smaller building that said Best Reality above the door. The small building looked more like a glorified shack than a reputable business, and based on the name, Trey figured that it must have been a relative of Mrs. Best who also ran the real estate agency in town.

People must stay with Mrs. Best while they shop

for a home with one of her kids or something, he thought. *Who the fuck wants to live here though?*

Across the street was a large gray building with black moisture lines down the sides. It had tall glass windows that showed a variety of tools and appliances on one side of the door and advertisements for medications on the other. Jackson Hardware & Drug was painted in garish yellow letters across the windows. He chuckled at the quaintness of it and imagined some grandpa buying a hammer and some dick pills in the same transaction.

Trey crossed the street, noticing for the second time that there didn't seem to be any traffic lights in town, just an abundance of stop signs. While Main Street itself was mostly cleared of any signs of the forest, the rest of the town seemed to have the same towering firs that encircled Jackson Point sprouting from every conceivable place. Houses tilted from broken foundations, and sidewalks split from the tree roots that tried to take back what the loggers had stolen. And he had thought Portland had been a bastion of green.

From here, Main Street shifted from the businesses that greeted you on your way into town to a residential area with houses of various sizes. Some were old and clearly dated back to the founding of the town, while others looked more like manufactured homes dropped onto empty lots in the '80s.

Another block past the boarding house and Main Street unceremoniously ended with a faded sign that read: *Jackson Rd, Wahtum Lake 3 Miles.*

"That's it, huh?" Trey wondered aloud. In the distance, Mount Hood towered over them, its white peak looking awfully inviting to him. He wished he could have been there instead of here. But snowboarding wouldn't revitalize his podcast or jump-start his literary career.

Still unwilling to look at his phone, Trey turned back around and decided to follow 5th Street to the East. Peeking out above the houses, he thought he could see one of the larger buildings in town, and he aimed to see what it was. Partway down the block, he realized that he was looking at the single school in Jackson Point, which served all 93 students: Rachel Jackson Memorial School. Named for the wife of President Andrew Jackson, who seemed to have been an obsession of the town's founder.

To his right was a small drive-through burger stand blandly called Happy's Burgers. Ignoring the renewed hunger pangs and what they might mean, Trey ignored the burger stand and continued his brisk pace past the school. It was a large blue building that seemed to have been cobbled together over various decades. On the far end was what could have once been a church steeple, and the closest side to him looked more in line with a modern high school auditorium.

"That's where Kevin Anderhoff is right now," he sighed.

The embarrassment still hadn't faded. He had been lured to this backwater with the promise of breaking new ground in the True Crime field by…a child. Even so, the old woman seemed to think that her grandson had lured Trey into something dangerous, so he hoped that meant the whole thing wasn't some kind of a joke.

A man of Trey's age jogged by, his junk bouncing around in shorts. The sight made Trey uncomfortable, but also unable to look away. The man nodded in greeting.

"Check your roots," he said cheerfully and continued on his way.

What the hell does that mean? Trey thought.

Behind the school was another intersection, with the northern street being Eichle Avenue and Fifth turning into another country road named Wacum. Trey turned left and followed Eichle up another block before wandering toward a break in the trees. After another few minutes of walking and a couple of turns, he was standing in front of an expansive cemetery that seemed to stretch a few hundred yards into the distance where it abutted against the trees.

The front of the cemetery was fenced with wrought iron that terminated in two red brick pillars with a metallic arch between them. The arched sign read: *Manifest Destiny Cemetery*. Trey shook his head silently. Emblazoned on one of the pillars were the words: Our Roots Run Deep, To Where She Sleeps. He bowed his head in mock reverence and trundled into the graveyard.

The headstones that filled the cemetery were mostly squat and square, though some towered above him with stone-wrought angels or hooded figures leering down at him. More still had leaves or tree branches emblazoned on them. The ground was uneven throughout as if the trees that bordered the graveyard were reaching hungrily for those buried beneath his feet. He felt a sudden chill at the thought and wrapped his arms around his chest. He should have grabbed his coat.

Towards the middle of the cemetery were several rows of white folding chairs in front of a podium shaded by a canvas tent. Beside the podium was the picture of a young man who couldn't have been more than 20 years old. There was no casket laid out yet, but the grave itself seemed to have been dug already.

"Sad story," a deep voice intoned from behind Trey, making him jump.

Trey turned around and nodded at the old man who stood in front of him. The man was worse for wear, his blue coveralls stained with dirt and mud. He leaned on a shovel and grinned at Trey with a smile that was missing more than one tooth.

"I'm sorry," Trey said. "I didn't mean to intrude. I'm visiting and I just wanted to walk around town. I find cemeteries...peaceful."

"Aye, me too," the man said, extending a hand, "that's why I took this job. The name's Alistair McCabe, gravedigger, undertaker, and funeral director."

Trey took that man's hand. His grip was firm, but his skin felt cool and almost wet.

"I'm Trey Savage. That's a lot of hats for one man to wear."

"It is, it is," Alistair replied with a wink. "But that's the way of the small town. Not enough work for more than one man, but too much work for just one." He laughed in a deep rumble that seemed suited to a much larger man.

"What-uh-what happened to this kid?" Trey asked.

"Ain't that why you're here?" Alistair asked.

"Excuse me?"

"We don't get visitors in Jackson Point. So I

figured that means you came on account of the murders?"

Trey felt himself relax. For a moment, the thought that the man actually knew who he was had startled him.

"Well, yes. I'm a podcaster and a writer, so I came here to do a story on the murders. I was told that there had been five?"

"Podcaster?" the man said quizzically.

"I—uhm—I'm a journalist," Trey replied, trying to sound more official than he felt.

"I see, I see. Yes, there were five, but now Chance here makes six. Ate up like the others, too. Though you didn't hear that from me, no, you didn't."

"So…they *have* been eaten? Parts of them, I mean?"

"Look, *Trey*," Alistair began, looking around suspiciously, "I don't want no trouble. People die here all of the time, and I just put 'em in the ground to nourish the roots, see? If I was you, I'd leave it at that. Have a good day now, the service is at 7."

Alistair shouldered past Trey, his previous smile replaced with a grimace.

"One more question, Mr. McCabe," Trey said after the man.

Alistair stopped but didn't turn around.

"When did he die?"

"Two days ago," the gravedigger replied before continuing on. "They found him Wednesday morning, right about this time."

Trey felt his stomach drop. He mumbled a thank you and turned back toward the entrance to the cemetery. When he felt that he was far enough from the gravedigger, he picked up his pace and nearly ran back out to the street. *Wednesday! Wednesday!*

Fumbling for his pocket, Trey pulled out his phone and looked at the date.

Friday, October 18th.

The scone and coffee splattered the sidewalk right in front of Manifest Destiny Cemetery. Trey was too shaken to stop and even make a cursory attempt at cleaning it up. He continued his brisk pace up the street and cut across Fourth back towards Main. He needed to lie down. Perhaps some rest would help him remember where the time had gone. Then in the afternoon, he would find this Kevin and see what he had gotten himself into.

4

Kevin Anderhoff sat at the back of his classroom, trying to melt into the wall. There were only 8 other students in the room with him, but twice that number of desks, which allowed him to isolate himself as an island alone against the back wall, though his dark clothing immediately set him apart from the rest. He brushed his long, artificially black hair out of his eyes to get a better view of his teacher.

Ms. Moore was teaching this period, and she always made Kevin feel a mix of emotions. She was one of the few faculty members who was actually nice to him, almost in a sisterly kind of way. Which was the problem. Ms. Moore—Samantha was a Black woman who grew up outside of Jackson Point. Her hair was done up in braids that she had twisted into a bun. She was gorgeous, but was also looked at funny by nearly every white person in town—which was almost everyone. Her taking an interest in keeping Kevin safe was great and all, but also a source of more derision from his classmates. Ms. Moore also had a nice rack that he secretly hoped would bust loose from her button-downs. That was no way to think of his favorite teacher.

"The Watlala Tribe," Ms. Moore continued, "spoke a dialect of Chinook…"

Someone in the room made a whooping noise that drew a dark look from the teacher.

"Gerald, you are staying after class. You know I don't have patience for that racist bullshit."

The rest of the class "oohed" like they always did when she swore. If anyone was offended by her sometimes-coarse language, no one had thought to report her. Not that it would have done much good. Who wanted to teach here anyway?

"As I was saying," she continued.

Kevin drifted off, sketching on his notepad while a hidden earbud sat snug in his left ear under the mop of his greasy black hair. An episode of his favorite podcast, *The Dead and the Undead*, played at a volume just loud enough to drown out the lecture, on that side at least. This episode was an old one, there weren't any new ones recently, but Kevin didn't mind. He'd listened to each episode more than once, even when they came out weekly. But now, Trey, the host of the show, was on a hiatus to go and investigate a crime himself, thanks to a listener tip. That listener had been Kevin.

Kevin straightened and let his pencil rest. This episode was getting to the good part.

The men had been dismembered in an orderly fashion. First, they had been gutted from throat to groin, with their insides cleaned out like a fisherman would do to a fresh catch. Then their arms and legs had been sawed off at the joints before being cut into even smaller, more manageable pieces. Those were stored in coolers along the floor of the barn while the torsos hung from the rafters on meat hooks.

Every single officer who had been first on the scene resigned after the case was closed. Most won't talk about what they found in that barn—and at least one was known to have committed suicide in the months following the conviction.

Why did Henry Ames Bekker butcher those men? No one knows for sure. He never confessed or explained a single detail of his crimes, maintaining his innocence until his death. Some five years into his six consecutive life sentences, Bekker chewed off each of his own fingers in the night and bled out before he was discovered by the prison guards in the morning. During the autopsy, they found all ten fingers in his stomach.

If that wasn't scary enough for you, I leave you with this: the heads of the dead men were never re-covered. Nothing except a single tooth from one of the victims, which was found on the edge of the forest behind the barn.

This episode had been a series of short vignettes about serial killers who did unspeakable things and never once admitted to why. Trey postulated earlier in the episode that these men could have been possessed by a Demon or some other malefic entity at the time of their crimes. Though Kevin knew the host well enough by this point to guess that the suggestion wasn't genuine. *If only he'd grown up here*, Kevin thought distantly.

He looked down at his paper and realized that he had been drawing a headless and arm-less corpse while listening to the story. Quickly scribbling, Kevin covered most traces of his macabre doodle. The furiousness with which he did this attracted the attention of Ms. Moore.

"Kevin!" she snapped, though not with the same gruffness that Gerald had received, "Are you daydreaming again? I'll talk to you after class, too."

"Yes, Sam—I mean Ms. Moore," Kevin muttered.

He ignored the handful of snickers and went back to staring intently at his paper. By now, Trey was discussing his sponsor again and giving a snippet of next week's episode. He mentioned that he would do a deep dive on whichever killer from this episode won a popularity poll on his website. Kevin intended to let the podcast roll onto the next episode when he remembered something that Trey had said earlier.

Fumbling with his phone in his pocket so he didn't draw Ms. Moore's attention again, Kevin rewound the podcast to the middle. This was when Trey had mentioned the possibility that these serial killers were acting on behalf of an outside entity.

Take, for example, Kenneth Knox, the Capital Cannibal. Knox was convicted of killing some thirteen girls between the ages of six to sixteen. What set Knox apart from others of his ilk was both the murder weapon and the lack of signs of sexual sadism involved.

Knox killed each of the girls using nothing other than his teeth. I'll repeat that for those who missed it. Kenneth Knox killed thirteen young girls by literally eating them alive. In the process, there was no sign that he sexually abused them in any way.

This was not the work of a murderous pedophile, but something far stranger.

During his trial, where he was convicted after DNA evidence pulled from Knox's toothbrush matched an oral swab taken at the time of his arrest, he claimed complete and total innocence. That's not that uncommon—what is uncommon, though, is that Kenneth Knox was the one who turned himself in to the police as a potential suspect.

You see, Kenneth had been having horrific nightmares that involved, you guessed it: cannibalism. One day, when he awoke, he found a scrap of flesh between his teeth and immediately called the police. While on the surface that sounds more like a guilty conscience than anything, consider that Knox maintained his innocence during and after the trial, even though he turned himself in for 'possible involvement without his knowledge'.

Knox was executed by the state of Alabama via the electric chair in 1997. It was said that while he was being strapped down, he claimed once more that he did not do this, before promptly laughing and speaking in a foreign language. Before they could get the leather strap in his mouth, Knox had chewed off his own tongue.

Prior to the killings, and in the decades since, not one allegation has come out about Knox, sexual or otherwise. He was always known to be polite, outgoing, good with kids, and a lover of animals. Not once had he ever shown any signs of being a serial killer.

Was Knox possessed by the Devil? No doubt some religious quarters have postulated exactly that. I propose the theory that each killer mentioned in this episode could have fallen under the sway of some other 'entity', Satanic or otherwise. Why would I think this, the skeptic that I usually am? Consider this last detail about the Knox case: at each crime scene, these words were written in the victims' blood: We Eat Our Children, Just As They Ate Theirs.

That was it. Kevin realized why this part had popped back into his brain even though he had glossed over it the first time. He needed to see if Trey had checked in yet or not. That meant getting through this conversation with Ms. Moore as quickly as possible.

🐚

"It won't happen again," Kevin said, trying desperately not to stare at her chest.

"That's what you said last week, Kevin," she sighed, crossing her arms. Did she realize where he had been looking?

"I-I've just been so distracted by what's been going on and—" Kevin began.

"Shh," Ms. Moore said, placing a finger over her lips. "I know it's hard, but you pay that no mind. The more we talk about it, the more we possibly draw her eye, you understand? Watch where you dig."

"And check your roots," Kevin replied.

"Do you have a shift at Happy's Burgers tonight?" she asked, moving to sit behind her desk.

"No ma'am."

"Good. Then get home and get ready for the funeral. I'll see you there?"

"Yes, ma'am."

Kevin smiled weakly before darting out of the room. He knew that she was just looking out for him, but he couldn't allow all of the adults in town to keep ignoring the fucked-up shit that happened around here. He couldn't. That's why he had tried to get outside help. That's why he had reached out to the best expert he could think of: Trey Savage.

5

Trey awoke that afternoon with a pounding headache. He sheepishly went downstairs to ask Mrs. Best for some Ibuprofen and the Wi-Fi password. It was nearly 3 PM, so he knew that he should expect a visit from Kevin sometime soon unless this whole thing turned out to be some kind of twisted prank, which he still hadn't ruled out.

Sitting at the desk, he booted up his laptop and connected to the boarding house's Wi-Fi, aptly named: Best Wi-Fi. While there was internet of a sort here, it moved at a snail's pace, like the DSL modem speeds of his early childhood. He guessed that was because the whole town probably used some kind of rural satellite-based internet connection that was as fickle as the weather. The first thing he did was check his email and confirm that he wasn't crazy—or at least not in *that* way.

He had booked his check-in for Monday evening, the 14th. Which meant that if it really was the 18th, he had shown up some four days late, and there was no way that could have happened. Sure enough, his last messages sent out to friends back home, as well as the last purchase made with his debit card, which had been for gas in Cascade Locks, had all been on the 14th.

"So what the fuck happened to the rest of this week?" he sighed.

Somebody had to be messing with him. But how had they changed the date on his phone? He looked online, and everything he looked at confirmed that it was the 18th now, not the 15th like he knew it should have been. Was it possible that he had passed out on Jackson Road and didn't realize it? There was no way he could have slept through nearly four days, checked in, and not had the woman or her grandson wondering why he had been late.

Even though his headache was now considerably worse, he slammed his laptop shut, threw on his coat, and grabbed his backpack for the second time that day. He wouldn't sit around waiting for this *kid* to show up. He had a case to cover. Hell, he had a case to *solve*.

The shadows had begun to stretch from the left side of the street to the right as he traveled north up Main Street. Although it wasn't that late in the afternoon, being nestled between mountains and tucked away in a forest seemed to make the daylight hours much shorter.

What was it she warned me of last night? He thought. *Being out after dark means you could feed the Rootmother or something?*

He had covered a lot of local legends and superstitions with his podcast over the years. But unlike the true crime aspect of the show, the supernatural lore never grabbed him the same way. He found it fascinating, sure, in the way a good ghost story can be entertaining, but he never believed any of that shit. To Trey, it was like telling scary stories around the campfire, it's just that half of them were true. Thinking about being in an active serial killer's hunting ground caused him to shiver. He wanted to be the one telling the stories, not someone trapped in them.

Once he was farther up the block, Trey had to choose between the police station and the library. He didn't expect that the local cops would be super forthcoming with some outsider journo, so he crossed the street and ran up the steps that led to the Frederick Ansel Library.

The building was a large brick and marble structure, a library in the classic sense. On either end of the stairs sat two large stone figures that looked like trolls or some kind of tree sprites. They resembled old men made out of bark, and each held a creepy rictus grin.

He pushed through the glass doors and entered the sprawling complex. It was difficult not to have a sense of awe at the structure. There was no reason for a town like this to have a library of this size, or even a library at all, really. He felt like he had walked into a library in New York City or somewhere, not some backwater in Oregon.

The foyer was cavernous, with shining marble floors and high, arched ceilings. The walls were adorned with oil paintings of people Trey didn't recognize, and landscapes—some of which looked familiar and some of which looked downright alien. Trey walked past the paintings, making a mental note to study them closer at a later time, and walked to the front desk.

The desk was a massive thing, nearly fifteen feet long. Behind it stood rows and rows of old card catalog drawers and filing cabinets of various sizes. A placard above hung from a chain just over the desk that read: *Knowledge For All, Knowledge From One.* A brass bell sat on the desk, and no one was visible, so Trey tapped the bell and gritted his teeth as the *ding* rang out through the silence of the library.

A few moments later, a door slammed somewhere in the distance. He tried to see where it had come from, but all he could see were rows and rows of towering shelves. Beyond that, spiral stairs that led up to another level. He whistled aloud in spite of himself.

"Can I help you?" a woman asked.

Startled, Trey spun and saw an older man standing behind the desk. The man wore a small pair of spectacles over a bulbous nose that nearly obstructed his thick mustache. Trying not to show his surprise at the man's sudden appearance, Trey leaned in and placed an elbow on the countertop.

"Hi," Trey said. "I'm new here, and I'm planning to do some research. Could you point me in the right direction? And do I need a library card?"

The Librarian leaned in toward Trey and pointed up at the placard.

"*All* doesn't mean only those with a library card."

"Ah, yes, of course," Trey stammered. "I'd like to look at local history, and the newspapers you have as well."

The man eyed him suspiciously before speaking, "Periodicals are on the ground floor toward the back, section F, near the reading tables. Town history is on the second floor, section A."

The librarian turned away and gave a huff, meaning that the conversation was over. Trey decided not to mumble a thanks this time and hurried toward section F. He would tackle the papers first, and the town history second. He needed to find out just what was being said about these murders in the local media before he went hounding the police. Then he would learn a little more about Jackson Point—if for no other reason than to put his mind at ease about the missing days.

The section labels were written on lacquered signs that hung from the darkness of the ceiling by dainty chains. Again, he felt that the very existence of this place was at odds with the town itself. *Maybe there's something about that in the town's history?*

Sure enough, the newspapers and magazines that made up the periodical section were toward the back under a hanging sign that simply read: *F.* Tables and chairs were scattered about this area as well, though each of them had enough dust to imply extreme disuse. The newspapers themselves were against the left wall; newer editions hung open from horizontal wooden poles to keep their shape, while copies older ones were stacked in cubbies that lined the walls—no scans here, it seemed.

Trey thumbed through the newer papers looking for something local, but he couldn't find anything local to Jackson Point. He started looking through the papers from other towns around the Gorge, but came up empty. Nowhere were the murders mentioned. Hell, Jackson Point itself was never even mentioned. It was like everyone else in this part of the state would rather pretend that the town didn't exist.

Just to see if he was right, Trey began flipping through the facsimile copies in the cubbies, going back as far as the 1850s edition of *The Oregonian*. After what felt like a few hours, he finally found one single reference to Jackson Point:

Thursday, October 14th, 1897

Jackson Point Mayor Found Dead

Sometime in the early hours of the morning, Frederick Ansel, self-proclaimed mayor of the logging community of Jackson Point, was found dead in his home. Ansel leaves behind no family, and his estate is already the subject of a legal battle for ownership of most of the town's business interests.

While details as to the cause of death are not yet known, it seems that Ansel was the victim of a vio-

lent homicide reminiscent of the Lizzie Borden case from Massachusetts five years ago.

And that was it. One small article, barely two paragraphs long, about a murder. How could there be so little? Even in this case, the violent murder of the mayor should have amounted to more than two simple paragraphs.

Trey read the article again to see if he missed something. He had, and seeing it caused his blood to run cold.

Thursday, October 14th, 1897

The mayor had been killed on October 14th. The same day that Trey was supposed to have checked in at the boarding house. The same day that he started to lose time. While it was clearly just a coincidence, it didn't make him feel any better. Feeling like he had been poring over the papers too long, he hastily put them back—but not before snapping a picture of the article with his phone—and quickly made his way to the nearest staircase.

As he ascended to the second floor, he felt as if each of his footfalls echoed throughout the building. He wouldn't have been surprised to find out that he and the single librarian were the only souls in the entire structure. That thought brought him no comfort either. Halfway up the steps, he considered turning back and going to look for Kevin. Chastising himself for being a baby, he trudged up to the second floor.

The shelves here were shorter than on the ground floor, but no less dense. This facility must have held hundreds of thousands of books dating back to the town's founding or even before. He looked at the walls of titles without taking the time to really read any of them. Most of the books on this level appeared to be old. Spines with golden letters sagged on the shelves, covered in the dust of decades. Spiders and other things crawled along the tops of the books just out of the light that shined from naked bulbs above.

Section A loomed ahead, once more at the rear of the building. If he hadn't asked, nothing would have clued him in that this was local history. He started by scanning the titles of the oldest-looking volumes and worked his way to the present. While most of the books were about the Columbia River Gorge in specific, and Oregon history more broadly. Finally, though, he found the books about Jackson Point itself. It seemed that someone, at least, wasn't pretending this town didn't exist.

He pulled down two dusty leather tomes: *Jackson Point: A History of Blood and Sap*, and *Fred-*

erick Ansel: The Man Who Conquered the Gorge.
Trey looked around for a table and found one
tucked away in the corner where two shelves
terminated.

Gingerly, he set the two books down and
started flipping through them, making notes in
his Moleskine or snapping pictures when neces-
sary. While the history of the town itself might
have been fascinating, Trey only cared about it
inasmuch as he could provide texture to his
book and podcast about the murders. If such a
brutal killer as Kenneth Knox was operating in a
community of only 1,500 people, it stood to
reason that there would be some interest in the
history of the town itself.

Originally, it seemed that Jackson Point was a
logging camp founded by the Hudson Bay Company somewhere around 1830, a few years after
they founded Fort Vancouver to the west. Sometime in that interim, a man named Frederick
Ansel, once an employee of the very same
Hudson Bay Company, took over the financing
of the lumber operation using his own funds.
The area that became Jackson Point was chosen
because the trees seemed to grow better here,
and loggers claimed that trees cut down one day
would be back the next.

Trey glossed over the next drier sections
about the camp becoming an unofficial town

and the resistance by "Mayor" Frederick Ansel to incorporate following Oregon's statehood. When he did stop again, it was when the book made a passing reference to the murder of Ansel, sharing even less information than *The Oregonian* article had. Frustrated, Trey flipped to the biography and jumped to the back, hoping to pick up on some of the gorier details.

"I wouldn't be reading books like that out here," a woman said quietly.

For the second time since coming into the library that day, Trey nearly jumped out of his skin. A dark-haired and dark-eyed woman towered over him. She wore a pleated brown skirt and a white blouse with ruffles that reminded him of the bedspread from the boarding house. Her face was soft, but her eyes were hard. She had one hand on her hip as she glowered at him with pursed lips. The woman looked to be close to his age, though he couldn't really tell in the poor lighting up here.

"Excuse me?" Trey asked, trying not to continue looking her over too thoroughly.

"I said, you shouldn't be reading books like that out in the open," she replied. "It's bad enough that you asked Herman where to find them, but then you don't even take them to a reading room?"

"I'm sorry, miss...I don't—" he began.

"No, that's the problem with you outsiders, you don't understand. There are people in this town who won't take kindly to seeing you reading books like this, so I'd recommend doing your research in one of the private reading rooms."

"Of course, of course," Trey stumbled over himself to say. He grabbed the books and threw his bag back over his shoulder. "Those would be?"

"Follow me," she said with an exaggerated sigh.

She led him across the second floor to a series of doors on the far wall. Above the doors were the faded words that said: *Reading Rooms,* and below that: *Please turn off the lights when you are done.*

With a huff, the woman opened one of the doors and nearly shoved Trey inside. The room was very small, with a square table and two chairs resting against opposite walls. It smelled like dust and old paper inside. And perfume. Trey swallowed hard as he looked at the woman, who was now standing inches away from him.

"When you're done, shut the lights off and kindly put the books back where you found them. The fewer people who know you were reading them, the better."

She turned to go, and Trey stopped her with

a hand on her shoulder. The woman reflexively jerked away from him.

"Oh sorry," he muttered. "What's your name?"

"Becca," she said as the door closed behind her.

Trey slumped down into one of the chairs and stared at the two books for a long time, but he couldn't bring himself to open them. His mind was stuck on other things for the time being.

6

"Where have you been?" the pasty teenager exclaimed.

Trey had just walked through the door of the boarding house, and already he was being accosted by some kid. Outside, the sun had truly begun to set, shading the town gray and black. The kid in front of him couldn't have been more than sixteen. A lanky, pale-skinned boy with moody black hair and black nail polish to match his clothing. The kid's face was a warzone of zits and the scars that came from picking at them.

"You must be Kevin," Trey said with a sigh.

"Yes, I am. You had me freaking out. I've been waiting here since I got out of school."

"Look, Kevin, I appreciate the tip, but—"

"Not here!" Kevin hissed. "Up in your room. Come on."

Kevin led the way as if he were the one staying there and not Trey. The stairs didn't seem to creak as much under the boy's weight as they did Trey's, as if the house welcomed him more than the outsider. *This place is getting to me already.*

When they got to the room, Kevin barreled inside and slammed the door shut behind Trey without a word. The boy pulled out the desk chair and sat with a soft thump, crossing his arms in front of his chest. His eyes frantically searched the room like he was an animal caught in a hunter's trap. Trey awkwardly sat on the bed and raised his hands in a placating gesture.

"Look," he began, slowly this time in case he was cut off again. "I appreciate the tip, I really do. And it means a lot to me that you are a fan, but I didn't know you're a kid and—"

"I'm not a kid," Kevin protested.

"Okay then, how old are you?"

"I'm...sixteen or seventeen. It's hard to remember. Time is...look, it doesn't matter. There is something more going on here than just a serial killer."

Trey stared at the boy in disbelief. He didn't know how old he was? Just like Trey didn't know what happened for nearly four days since coming to this godforsaken place.

"What was that you said about time? I was

supposed to check in on the 14th, right? I know you run your grandma's email account. Anyways, the 14th? So that's the day I left, Monday. But when I woke up this morning, it was Friday. What the hell is going on?"

Kevin sighed and looked out the window. The street lamps started to kick on in rapid succession as the last scattered orange beams of the sun flickered out. Before the boy turned back around to speak, the wind started to rattle the shutters on the outside of the house.

"I-I'm sorry I brought you here," he said, barely above a whisper. "This place isn't safe."

"Yeah, no shit!" Trey laughed for the first time all day. "There's a serial killer on the loose in a town of little over a thousand people. I'd be safer swimming with sharks."

The boy looked irritated. His face scrunched up so tightly that Trey worried he was going to hurt himself.

"That's not what I meant. Look, there *is* more going on here than just a serial killer, okay? The missing days you mentioned? Get used to that. Time is, it's…it's broken here. Always has been, since before any white dudes showed up. Local tribes stayed the hell away, and we should have too. Once you get here, it's like a vortex that you can't leave, and I pulled you into it and I—"

"Kid, calm down," Trey said dismissively.

"Look, again, glad you're a fan of the show, but—and I can't stress this enough, the 'undead' portion of *The Dead and the Undead* is mostly just BS. Ghost stories and local legends. Shit that's cool and scary to talk about, but it isn't real, okay? I believe in real monsters, not the made-up kind that haunt graveyards."

Kevin was starting to look agitated again. It made Trey nervous. The last thing he needed was some goth kid freaking out and costing him his room.

"I know, okay!" Kevin exclaimed, leaning in so his voice didn't carry by mistake. "I know you don't buy the supernatural shit on your show. I can tell. I've listened to every one of your episodes since I was a kid. I wouldn't either, if I didn't live here. You said it yourself, you lost several days, and I bet if you mentioned it to anyone else, they'd act like you were just confused, yeah?"

Trey nodded in spite of himself.

"And I bet that you've already had some people say some weird shit to you? Tell you not to ask or talk about stuff? Not to go out after dark?"

Trey nodded again, a cold sweat breaking out just between his shoulders.

"That's because there is something controlling this town. I don't know what it is. Most people here don't. But they also know not to talk about it, or they might end up dead or thrown into a padded cell in the hospital basement. To us kids, it seems like stupid superstitions that old people tell when they've only lived in one place their entire lives. 'Rootmother take you' and all that nonsense. But there's something behind it! Something that breaks time. Something that feeds the trees. Something that killed Chance Bainbridge and all the others."

Kevin was breathing hard now, clearly having used all of his courage to tell off one of his idols. Trey sat in silence for a few minutes, processing everything the boy had said. When the silence became too hard to bear, he finally broke it.

"Okay, let's say you're onto something," Trey began, once again holding his hands up to the boy. "Why me? What did you think I could do about it? I'm no cop. Hell, I'm barely a journalist. I'm a fucking podcast host whose show is hemorrhaging listeners while I'm trying to cash in with a book."

Kevin looked truly deflated for the first time since he sat down.

"I-I don't know," he said quietly. "I just felt like I needed to do something, I needed somebody to help. Someone from the outside who would listen. Maybe together we could figure out what is doing this and—"

"And what?" Trey cut in. "And stop them? Look at me, Kevin. I'm not an action hero, I've never even held a gun for Chrissakes. I'm. A. Podcaster. Sure, I'd like to think I could 'solve the case' and whatnot, but I never intended to be the one to bring the guy in."

Kevin's eyes lit up.

"You might have already solved it," he said, jumping to his feet. "In episode #256, the one about killers who claimed they didn't do it, right up to the end, you said that they might have been possessed by some other entity."

"Yeah, I remember," Trey said morosely. "I said that these killers could have been under the sway of something else. That they themselves held no actual accountability for the crimes? It was bullshit, Kevin. I was just saying spooky shit for the show. Kenneth Knox? He was a fucking nutjob who wanted to have those girls inside of him instead of the other way around. Henry Ames Bekker was a rancher and butcher who started carving guys up the same way he would a hog. Michael Faust was—"

"I know you don't buy it," Kevin interjected. "Like I said, I could tell even from the episode. But I think your 'theory', even if it was just bull-shit about the men in that episode, was right in this case. Whoever is doing this is under the sway of whatever entity controls the town. I think...I think these murders are actually sacrifices."

"Sacrifices to what?"

"The Rootmother," Kevin whispered. "She Who Sleeps Beneath the Trees."

Then there was a loud crash outside, and all hell broke loose.

Trey and Kevin took the stairs down two at a time, neither wanting to miss whatever had happened out in the street. A car alarm was blaring, and it sounded like a woman was screaming bloody murder. Down in the foyer, they ran past Mrs. Best, who was in a black dress with a veil over her face. Belatedly, Trey remembered that the funeral was less than an hour away.

"What's going on, Kevin?" she wheezed, her concern taking a toll on her oxygen level.

Both Trey and Kevin ignored her as they threw the front door open. Outside, the back of Trey's SUV was caved in. That was the source of the car alarm. The other car, a small sedan of some kind, was flipped over in front of Best Realty. A woman was trying frantically to pull a bloodied man out of the driver's seat. That was the source of the screaming.

Taking a millisecond to mourn his car, Trey

rushed over to the side of the screaming woman. The man in the car had lost a lot of blood already. It pooled inside the windshield and was puddling in the street amidst the broken glass where Trey and the woman knelt. Trey checked the guy's pulse, or at least tried to, and thought it seemed faint.

"Kevin!" he shouted over the car alarm. "Do you have a phone that works in this fucking place?! Call somebody!"

Kevin nodded and ran back inside. It may not have mattered as, already, folks were beginning to gather to see what the commotion was. Trey located the largest wound on the man's chest. He took off his coat and pressed it against the bloody gash.

"Hold this!" he shouted to the woman. "I'm gonna stop that fucking alarm so we can think, okay?!"

The woman nodded and placed her hands on the already-soaked jacket. Trey stood and fumbled around in his pockets with slick fingers. He pulled out his keys and tried the buttons to stop the alarm, but nothing worked. He rushed over to the driver's door and wrenched it open, popping the hood moments later. Then he disconnected the battery cables, and the night silence returned, broken only by the choked sobs of the woman at the other car. Running back to her, he placed his hands over hers to keep the jacket in place.

"It's okay," he said. "I've got it. Step back and take a breath."

"Trey!" Kevin shouted. "Sheriff Tench and Doctor Baker are on their way!"

"And why the hell aren't they here already?" Trey shouted back.

"They were probably getting ready for my son's funeral," the woman croaked.

"Oh," Trey said. "I'm so sorry."

❧

A few minutes later, both the Doctor, a heavyset guy in his forties, and the sheriff, a pixie-cut blond closer to Trey's age, showed up. The volunteer fire chief was there next, and together they got Mr. Bainbridge out of the car and on his way to the hospital. The hospital, Trey learned, was actually just a big-ass house that the Doctor lived in that also had some patient rooms.

The sheriff thanked Trey for his help keeping Mr. Bainbridge alive, but didn't say much else, instead shepherding Mrs. Bainbridge away from the accident. The funeral was supposed to begin in ten minutes, but the murmur in the crowd was that it should be canceled. That was when Mrs. Bainbridge started screaming.

"No! We have to bury him! We have to do it tonight, don't you see? We waited too long already, and now she's trying to take my husband, too! The roots need nourishment! We have to give him to the earth."

The sheriff put a tight arm around the woman and led her further from the crowd.

Kevin elbowed Trey in the ribs and gave him a knowing look. Trey swallowed hard and tried to avoid the teen's gaze.

"She's right!" a loud voice boomed. "We should still bury the boy. His mother needs closure, and, good-lord-willing, his father too. Everyone who was planning to attend, please head to Manifest Destiny, we will simply be starting late."

"That's the mayor," Kevin whispered to Trey. "You better come to the funeral with me."

As the pair walked toward the cemetery, Trey looked back at his car.

"I don't know where else I could go" he muttered.

7

The funeral began only thirty minutes later than was scheduled. The cemetery didn't normally have lights after dark, Kevin explained on the walk over, so some shop lights and a generator had been donated by the town mechanic, Dylan Purdy.

It seemed that more people were at the funeral than had been expected, for all of the chairs were taken and a small crowd stood in a half-circle behind them. Mrs. Best had been driven by her daughter Cynthia, Kevin's mom. They watched from Cemetery Road, where she could stay sitting in her daughter's luxury sedan. Trey and Kevin sat in the middle row of chairs. In front of them, Trey noticed Becca, the librarian from earlier, and he thought she was making a point to ignore him. On the other side of Kevin, a woman sat down whom Kevin greeted as Ms. Moore—she seemed to be one of his teachers.

Another Teacher patted Kevin on the shoulder as he walked past and took a knee beside the front row of chairs. This guy, Kevin called Mr. Nelson. Trey tried to make a mental note of each person who he caught the name of, thinking that any of them could have been the killer; SKs were known to visit the crime scenes or even memorials of their victims to relive the crime, after all. In a small town like this, it was very likely they would be at the funeral itself. Still, with the poor lighting at the cemetery, he was mostly making out silhouettes, not faces.

There was a coffin beside the podium now, a dark wood that shone like ebony in the faint light. Beside the coffin sat four chairs. The one closest to the dead boy was his mother, beside her, the chair was empty, and on the other side of that one sat both the mayor and the sheriff. Standing above everyone at the podium was a man whose age was hard for Trey to guess. He had thick hair that was going gray at the temples and a salt-and-pepper beard, but his face wasn't wrinkled like one would expect. He wore the garb of clergy and held an old leather bible in one hand and a gnarled root in the other.

"Welcome, brothers and sisters," the pastor intoned.

"Welcome, Shepherd Cabot," came the reply in unison.

"First, I would like to start with the good news, the news often spread by our savior Christ Jesus! The news of life!"

"Amen!" the crowd shouted.

"Will Bainbridge will be just fine. He suffered only minor injuries in the accident. The good lord has spared him!"

The crowd cheered and whooped at that. Trey had never seen so lively a funeral, but he expected that the news that they wouldn't be back here in a few nights, burying a father beside his son, was enough to raise some spirits.

"Now, as for Chance," Shepherd Cabot began, his voice somber. "We begin the process of returning him to the earth. To the *mother*."

For some reason, that last word made Trey wince.

"The Bible tells us not just of the return to the earth, but also of the resurrection. John 14 says 'Let not your heart be troubled: ye believe in God, believe also in me. In my Father's house are many mansions: if it were not so, I would have told you. I'm going to prepare a place for you. And if I go and prepare a place for you, I will come again, and receive you unto myself; that where I am, there ye may be also.'

"Is this not the truth, brothers and sisters? How much more so, for those of us who live in these blessed woods? Those of us who travel beneath the earth are reunited with our mother, and we shall be reborn again, in root and branch, sap and blood, bark and flesh."

"Amen!"

"Young Chance was taken from us before his time, but now he shall nourish our roots, feed our trees, shade our passing, and return to us in the days to come."

"Amen!"

"And to you I also say, take heart! There is a wickedness in our town now, it is true. Has it not taken six souls before their time? And yet, as the sword of the angels has fallen on the enemies of the Lord in the past, so too will our axe fall in judgment on the one responsible."

The crowd clapped and roared at this. Even Mrs. Bainbridge. Only Kevin and Trey sat quietly, it seemed. And Becca, Trey noticed.

"Now, let us commit this young man to the earth, and return him to the mother!"

Then the coffin was lowered into the hole dug earlier in the day by Alistair McCabe, and shortly thereafter, the crowd had dispersed and began heading back their separate ways. As they walked back to the boarding house, Trey tried to find the right words to say to Kevin.

"Did you know him well?" he croaked out, finally.

"Yeah," Kevin said. "He was my best friend since before school."

"Oh," Trey said sheepishly. "I'm sorry. I…it's just that you, well, none of you really seem as shaken up as I would have imagined with such a terrible crime having just happened. Especially to a friend of yours."

"Death is…different here," was all Kevin could say.

"Like time is?"

"Yeah, something like that."

When they finally got back to Best Boarding House, Kevin's mom was waiting for him in her car. He hopped in and waved goodbye to Trey. The sullen podcaster gave one last look at his destroyed car and went up to his room to write.

Trey pinned Becca against the wall in the reading room. Her blouse was undone, and her breasts were exposed. She bit his lip suggestively. He pressed her into the wall harder and then began sucking on her neck. She moaned. Softly at first, then loud enough that he was sure someone would hear.

She undid his pants and lifted her skirt. He felt her warmth with his fingers first, then he thrust himself inside of her. She cried out in ecstasy, clawing his back with acrylic nails. Pain and pleasure mixed until he could barely think straight.

When he was nearly finished, she sank to her knees and took him in her mouth, sucking and cupping and stroking until he was the one screaming. Just as he was about to climax, she bit down. He screamed again, but this time in pain rather than pleasure. She bit down even harder. He pulled back, but it was too late. Blood covered her face, and she was smiling.

❧

Trey sat bolt upright in bed. He had never had a sex dream like that before. He felt wetness in the sheets and chuckled a bit. He hadn't had a wet dream since high school. Sliding out of the wet sheets, Trey flipped on the light to see how messy it was. There was an extra set of bedding in the closet he could use if needed.

When his eyes adjusted to the brightness of

the room, he reflexively clamped a hand over his mouth to prevent himself from screaming. The bed wasn't wet from a nocturnal ejaculation but from blood.

8

This wasn't the first time it had awoken. Nor would it be the last. The cycle had started when the stars were young, and it would continue until they burned out. It hunkered on a fallen log, watching the men fell a tree below. All would feed the Elder One. All flesh would return to the earth.

It hunkered down on all fours and crept through the underbrush, careful not to be seen. If it weren't careful, this passage of the cycle would be finished, and that could not be. Not yet. One of the men stopped working and shouted something at the other. The second man sighed and pulled out a wooden tobacco pipe. The first man wandered off to relieve himself. It was pleased.

The sound of urine sprinkling the leaves of

ferns greeted its ears. It breathed deeply to take in the scent. It would feed again. It sprang from the bushes and gripped the man by the throat, stifling a yell. It didn't wait this time. It didn't wait for the air to leave the man's lungs. It tore his belly open with its teeth, spilling warm guts on the forest floor. Steam rose from the hot blood, splitting the mist that had begun to curl around their feet. The man no longer struggled. He shuddered a few more times and then went limp.

"Richard!" the other man called. "You taking a piss or a shit out there?"

It climbed the nearest tree and hung the man by his entrails. The branch groaned under his weight, but it held strong. His blood ran down the trunk of the tree to the roots. This was good. She would be pleased. The second man walked around the tree looking for the first. It landed on him with a wet crunch. It would get to feed again.

❦

The dreamer tumbled out of bed this time, landing on all fours on the floor. They shuddered at the sudden transition from sleep to waking. It was October 5th. That meant it had happened again. The others said this was good.

The others said that meant the cycle was continuing, just as it was supposed to. They weren't sure if they agreed.

After all, it was the dreamer who had the nightmares. It was the dreamer who awakened with the copper taste of blood in their mouth. And it was the dreamer who was killing the people of Jackson Point. They sighed and moved into the shower. The water was pink as the blood was washed away. The dreamer tried not to imagine whose blood it was. In a few hours, they would know.

9

Becca White opened the upper cabinet above her sink—the one with the sagging door. The almond-colored cabinets were all falling apart in one way or another, but the one that held her mugs was the saddest. She considered taking the door all of the way off, but never quite got around to it. No matter how hard she tried, she could never find the time.

The librarian pulled her favorite mug out; it had been handmade by Jenni before Becca had even turned sixteen. While she was trying to be cool and date the hottest guy in her class of twelve, her little sister had been playing with dolls and talking to her imaginary friend who lived under the trees. Then one day, Becca came home from school, and her sister had made this mug for her. She didn't appreciate it at the time, but now it was the only thing she had left of the three of them…

The nutty aroma of coffee tickled her nose just as the pot began to beep. She poured herself a cup and set the mug down on the counter. It didn't take more than a few seconds for the coffee to start to pool under the mug from where the heat had split it. Becca wiped away a tear and realized that she didn't know what time it was. The clock above her kitchen table was broken, forcing her to walk back to her bedroom and check her watch for the time.

"Fuck!" she exclaimed.

It was 8:59. Given that it was Wednesday, she was due at the library in sixty seconds. Evelyn would have her ass if she was late again. She overslept due to a dream about that outsider she met yesterday. It had started hot enough, but around the time he went down on her, things got…bloody. To make matters worse, she seemed to have started her period in the night—there was a little blood on the sheets.

Forgetting the coffee and Jenni's little smiling sun mug, Becca quickly threw on a skirt and blouse, slipped into her heels, and ran out the door. Moments later, she was back inside, grabbing her purse and phone, cursing again, and then slamming the door, for good this time.

Maybe next check, I can buy a new clock or an alarm I can't snooze, Becca thought.

The air was brisk this early in the morning, like it was every October. The steps of her trailer were slick with condensation from the nightly mist. Dodging the holes in the sagging stairs, she trudged out to the gravel drive that wrapped through Fallen Lilly's Trailer Park and powered her way toward the library. Her trailer was a gaudy pink with a rusted skirting that was buckling and falling down in more than one place. The other trailers in the park weren't much better—if you didn't inherit a house in Jackson Point, or like in Becca's case, your house burned down—this was where you ended up. For a moment, she wondered where that new guy would end up, if he lasted long enough. There was a trailer for rent at the back of the park, just two units down from hers. Of course, a city guy like him probably had the money to buy something a little nicer, and Lord knows that more than one house was vacant after the last month.

Fallen Lilly's was a short walk from the library, being only a block off of Main. On the rainy days, of which there were many, Becca would drive into work, but the rest of the time she tried to get her steps in, even if she was late. It was 9:16 when she finally made it behind the front counter and punched in using the 40-year-old time card machine.

Herman was pretending to flip through the card catalog when she came in. After hearing the loud punching of her time card, he turned on her and harrumphed. His eyes settled over her like a cat watching a mouse.

"Late again," he tittered. "Evelyn won't be happy with you, *Rebecca*."

Becca ignored him, grabbed the book cart, and pushed it past him without another word. That man made her all kinds of uncomfortable, but he was mostly harmless. Evelyn was likely in her office near the middle of the building. She would see that Becca was late soon enough. Maybe that was a good thing. Maybe that meant that she wouldn't ask questions that Becca didn't want to answer.

The returns today were fairly standard: some horror, some books about the Second World War, and a guide to birds in the Pacific Northwest. She made sure that when she bent over to examine the spines, her ass was pointed away from the main counter. There was no point in giving Herman something to drool over. One title did catch her eye, though: *Paganism & Pioneers* by J. B. French. This book wasn't ever checked out. In fact, it was on Evelyn's unofficial list of blacklisted titles that were supposed to be discouraged whenever possible.

Becca felt her palms begin to sweat as she ran her fingers down the worn blue spine. The dust jacket had long since decayed, leaving the blue cloth with faded white letters exposed. Who had checked this book out? Was it that outsider? Even after she warned him off? And if so, why did he return it already? Becca slipped the book down to the bottom shelf of the cart and made her way toward the horror section first. She hoped she could get the King and Hendrix books put away before seeing Evelyn, at least. That would give her time to think about why *Paganism & Pioneers* had ended up on her cart, today of all days.

The wheels of the cart broke the silence of the library with their rhythmic squeaking. Not for the first time did she think that they made it easy for someone to track her through the empty library. She shivered as she felt eyes on her back. Becca let one of the smaller books fall off the cart. Without missing a beat, she casually turned to pick it up, scanning the rows of shelves for the source of her discomfort. *Just Jackson Point*, she thought, when there was no one behind her. This town had a way of straining one's nerves.

Ahead, she made it to the horror section and started reshelving the returns. She made sure to flip through them as she did so to check for any lewd drawings made by the teens who often checked these books out. One time she found an illustration in the pages of *It* of the sewer orgy scene. That had been *quite* the phone call to the boy's parents.

As she was putting the books back, she pondered the book at the bottom of her cart. It was on her list of titles to read up on when she was free from prying eyes. Unfortunately, that wasn't often anymore since she had been caught reading *Those From the Stars* by Salem Kingsley, a treatise on the idea of ancient aliens visiting the earth in the millennia even before the dinosaurs. Evelyn had nearly fired her that day, prattling on about off-limit books and such.

"If these ones are so bad, why don't you keep them in your office with the other rare and restricted books?" Becca had asked.

That question had gotten her a two-day suspension without pay for insubordination. If any single thing about Jackson Point was true, it was that the older generation did not take kindly to questions. Keep your head down, check your roots, and watch where you dig. Becca tried later to come in on Evelyn's day off to look at the "off-limits" titles, but Herman had started watching her on the old woman's behalf. Since then, she had run out of ideas. Until that outsider showed up yesterday.

The squeaking of the cart began again as she rolled to the next section. The dim lights overhead swayed as if moved by some indoor wind. Becca took a deep breath to steady herself before rounding the corner that would put her directly in the line of sight of Evelyn's office. She knew that she wouldn't be lucky enough to avoid her boss this morning—things just weren't going her way so far.

Evelyn McReedy had been the head librarian at Frederick Ansel Library since before Becca was born. The woman looked to be in her eighties, yet she was still fit and spry as a woman in her middle age. Her office sat near the middle of the library, a room that's upper two-thirds was largely made of glass, to better give her a view of all of her domain. Her office also served as the true restricted section of the library. The sign above the door didn't actually say anything about being an office, but simply read: *Rare Book Room, library personnel only*. Which actually meant Evelyn McReedy only.

Evelyn was sitting at her desk, writing in her small red notebook. Her glasses, held to her head with a turquoise chain, slid down her beak-like nose. Her mouth was twisted up like she was sucking on something sour. As if she had a sixth sense, the old woman looked up from her note-book directly at Becca and motioned for her to enter the office with one crooked finger. Becca tried to put on her most disarming smile and pushed the cart, which now seemed to be squealing in panic, toward the door at the front of the office. She rolled the cart to a stop and reached for the door handle, realizing too late that she had left the cart with the spines facing the office. Becca hoped that the older librarian would be too busy chastising her to look closely at the bottom shelf.

The door creaked open, announcing Becca more clearly than any greeting could. She sat down on the single chair in front of Evelyn's desk and started smoothing her skirt. Lining the wooden half walls around them were shelves with books that Becca would have killed to have access to. Books like the Journal of Mathias Sabat, *The Elder Darkness*, *Revels of the Worm*, and other esoteric texts.

The older woman refused to look up for several agonizing minutes, though she did sigh and cough from time to time. Finally, she closed her red notebook with both hands and set it aside. Placing her elbows on the desk, she looked Becca over through steepled fingers.

"This is the third time that you've been late this year, Ms. White," she said. Her voice was gravelly like the Demon from *The Exorcist*. Becca attributed that to a lifetime of smoking, though she had never seen the woman even do so much as drink a glass of water.

"I'm sorry, Mrs. McReedy," Becca said in her politest-bitchy voice. "I didn't sleep well last night and—"

"This wasn't because of that outsider, was it?"

"Excuse me?" Becca tried to keep her mouth from hanging open.

"Herman told me that you spoke with that journalist who is in town yesterday. Did you not?"

So that's why he's here, Evelyn thought. She bit her lip to hide the smile that was starting to form.

"Yes, ma'am, I did. I directed him to our reading rooms."

"Did you talk to him about the...subject matter of the books he had chosen to read?" Evelyn asked with a stony look.

"No, I didn't," Becca lied. "Not directly, in any case. What books was he reading?"

Evelyn took off her glasses and rubbed the lenses with her sleeve. When she placed them back on the bridge of her nose, she was looking past Becca at the book cart.

"I don't know the exact titles, mind you. But Herman said he was asking about *Local History*.

You know how I feel about many of those books. Need I remind you that one of our jobs as the stewards of knowledge in this town is to steer people in the right direction? In many cases, that means *away* from certain titles, as I have done with you in the past."

Becca nodded silently. She was starting to sweat again as she followed the older librarian's eyes. Though she didn't say anything, Evelyn kept looking at the spines on the cart.

"It doesn't matter. I can't imagine he will be of concern long, especially if he keeps poking around. Be that as it may, I would prefer that you don't fraternize with him...for your own sake. Now, back to work."

"Yes, Mrs. McReedy," Becca said, standing.

She turned and placed her hand on the doorknob when Evelyn cleared her throat to get her attention. Becca turned back, masking her expression one final time.

"Don't be late again, Ms. White," Evelyn said with a hint of malice. "There aren't many jobs left in Jackson Point. I don't want to see you on the street. You know that wouldn't be safe..."

Becca nodded again, stiffer this time, and then fled the office as quickly as she could without drawing another comment from the old woman. She placed her shaky hands on the cart and started pushing it again. The wheel whined from the exertion, but Becca was able to get out of sight of that old bitch for the time being.

The rest of the books went back on the shelves with little fanfare. All except the one on the bottom. She thought about where to put it. It belonged in the U.S. History section, but something gave her pause. If the outsider was a journalist, then that meant he was here because of the murders. He was here to figure out what was going on in this town, and Becca aimed to help him find out, even if it killed them both. She owed Jenni that much, at least.

Angling the cart away from U.S. History, Becca moved toward the rear of the library near the periodicals. She opened the metal gate that blocked the freight elevator and pushed the cart inside. Once the gate was closed behind her, she thumbed the button for the second floor and took a deep breath. It seemed a small thing, to misshelf a book, but in Jackson Point it could have been a death sentence. No one would ever say that out loud, but somehow she knew.

The elevator clattered to a stop on the second floor, swaying on its cables for a few moments before the gate could be opened again. Becca pushed the cart to the Local History section, where she had found the outsider yesterday. She placed the book on the shelf next to the biography of Frederick Ansel and started to walk away. She checked her watch and saw that it was just past 10:30. The hook was baited, and now she just had to wait.

Another thought overtook her—one that was even more dangerous than placing that book in the wrong place. Becca quickly walked over to one of the reading rooms, trying to push the memories of her dream from her mind, and grabbed a scrap of paper and a pencil. She scribbled her phone number on it and returned to the shelf so that she could slip it into the book. As she pulled *Paganism & Pioneers* out, the book flipped open to a random page. There was already a scrap of paper there. She turned the paper over and saw the same ten digits that were on the paper in her hand. The hurried and squished numbers were her handwriting, too. Without realizing it, she lost her grip on the book, and it dropped to the ground. The thump reverberated across the second floor.

It was happening again. *Just like with Jenni.*

10

Trey hardly got any sleep the rest of that night. He lay awake for hours, staring at the bloody pile of sheets in the corner. When he finally did drift off, he mercifully didn't dream. In the morning, he rolled out of bed and checked his parts to make sure that they were still there. Satisfied that he hadn't been orally castrated in his sleep, he carried the sheets down to the washing machine on the first floor without running into Mrs. Best.

Once the laundry was going, he went back upstairs to shower and change. He needed to go see the mechanic first and foremost to see if his car could even still be driven home. If so, he would contact a body shop when he was done... which probably meant that he should have exchanged insurance information with the Bainbridge family last night. *Fuck!* Well, he could do that today, too. Then it was time to actually start looking into these murders. Something weird was going on with this town, but he planned to ignore it, no matter what Kevin told him.

After his shower, Trey got dressed in a simple black tee and jeans, skipping the flannel this time. Rather than bringing his whole backpack for note-taking, he slipped his mini-recorder into his pocket. Unlike the previous morning, where he felt like he hadn't eaten in days, Trey felt overly full like he had just waddled out of a breakfast buffet. Skipping the coffee so that he could dodge Mrs. Best again, he ducked through the front door and out into the street. His car was sitting in the same place, its rear end obliterated from the accident the night before.

Even though it was Saturday, Trey hoped that the mechanic would be open, at least for a few hours. He turned north and started back toward the only way into Jackson Point. As he passed the library, he thought he saw a glimpse of Becca slipping through the door. The sight of her dark hair and pale legs disappearing into the large building nearly caused him to stumble off the sidewalk. He tried to imagine the first part of his dream, and not the second.

Ahead, a pickup rolled through the stop sign on Main and 2nd, the driver eyeing him. Trey tried to wave, but the motion came across more like he was brushing the man off. The truck sped away, leaving a rolling plume of black smoke in its wake.

That Kevin kid must be crazy, Trey thought. *If this town really traps people, how the hell do they have all of these cars?*

He snorted for a moment when he thought about it. It was true that the people here were odd, to say the least, and they were under the shadow of a killer. But there wasn't anything *magical* going on. The missing days could be chalked up to exhaustion—and the bloody sheets? Well, that was probably the result of scratching an abscess or something in the middle of the night. Had to be. He had allowed his imagination to run wild and it was time to cut that shit out.

The town mechanic worked out of a large gray shop building that looked more like a warehouse than a public-facing business. On the far side was the solitary gas station aptly named Local Pump. Trey shook his head as he marveled at the naming conventions in this "town". *Hillbilly shit*, he thought again.

Trey trotted across the street and into the large garage door at the front of the shop. He could see the legs of a man sticking out from underneath the very sedan that had crushed his car the night before. The man didn't seem to have heard him walk up, so Trey cleared his throat and awkwardly shifted from one foot to the other while he waited for the guy to crawl out.

"Yup?" the man said in the form of a question.

"Yeah, uh, hi," Trey said, stretching out a hand. "I'm Treyton Savage. My SUV was the one that this car slammed into last night. I was hoping you could tow it in and see if it was still drivable."

"Yeah, I could do that once I'm done with the Bainbridge's here."

The mechanic looked like he was going to crawl back under the car when Trey stepped a little closer to stop him.

"There wasn't a sign outside," Trey said. "I'll need to know for when I call my insurance later."

The mechanic looked at Trey like he was an annoyance rather than a customer.

"Dylan," he said curtly as he climbed back under the car. "Don't have a name for the shop. Most folks just call it Dylan's."

"Okay then, Dylan," Trey said, dragging out the syllables. "Thanks again. I wasn't sure you'd even be open on a Saturday, to tell you the truth."

Dylan climbed back out from under the sedan to give Trey a confused stare.

"What're you talking about? It ain't Saturday, it's Wednesday."

Trey felt the blood drain from his face. He pulled out his phone and confirmed that it wasn't Saturday the 19th, but Wednesday the 16th.

"You alright, mister?" the mechanic asked.

"Fine. Yeah. Thanks."

Trey turned and tried to cross the street back toward the boarding house without panicking. He knew he wasn't losing his mind. Yesterday was Friday the 18th. The town had held a funeral for Chance Bainbridge—who had been found Wednesday morning. *This morning.*

Instead of going back to the Best, he turned and started running west down 2nd, looking for anything even remotely resembling a hospital. He had to find Will Bainbridge and ask him what had happened last night. Ask him what date last night even was.

What's going on? He thought. *This can't be fucking possible. There has to be an explanation. Everything can be explained. Everything.*

By the time he made it to a cross street named Brickle Ave, he still hadn't seen anything that would tell him where the hospital could be. Looking down Brickle, though, caused him to see something else that caught his eye. Not only did he see the General Store, but a large semi parked in front of it, with a man unloading freight for the store. Another person from out-side this crazy town.

He was practically sprinting now, and by the time he made it to the side of the truck, he was out of breath. The man unloading the truck had a blue uniform on, with an embroidered logo for some food company that Trey didn't immedi-ately recognize. He eyed Trey cautiously but didn't stop unloading his truck. Once Trey was done gasping for breath, he spoke.

"You aren't from around here, are you?" he asked.

"Nope," the driver replied, refusing to make eye contact.

"N-neither am I. Look, I have a few questions about this place. Uhm—do you come here often, do you make all of the deliveries to the store here?"

The driver finally stopped unloading and gave Trey a true once-over. His expression shifted from caution to pity.

"Yeah, I do. You said you aren't a local?"

"No, I'm not. I'm from Portland. Have you ever had anything weird happen here? Lost time?"

"I ain't never lost time here," the driver said, poking Trey in the chest, "because I ain't ever been here long enough to lose time, you understand? This place ain't right, and the longer you stay here, the worse it'll be for you."

"My car got smashed up last night," Trey said. "Could I maybe hitch a ride back with you, at least to Cascade Locks? I can call a friend—"

The driver turned and started unloading again.

"Nope. If you've been here that long, I want nothing to do with you. I'm not about to get stuck here."

"Stuck? What do you mean stuck? A town can't trap people, that's absurd."

"A town is a lot more than a collection of buildings," the driver said. "It's history, too. And this town has a whole mess of history I want no part of."

Trey stood his ground. He wasn't about to take no for an answer. He needed to get away from this place and clear his head. Maybe he just jumped into the deep end too fast. That had to be it.

"I'll pay you. Please, I need to get somewhere where my phone works."

"Ben! How's it going?" another voice shouted.

The driver put on a forced smile and turned away from Trey, waving at an older man who was walking out of the store.

"I've got a full load this time for ya, Eaton!

Why, I bet you could keep the whole town fed for the winter with this."

Deflated, Trey turned away from the two men and went back to wandering. That's when he saw the building, Kady Corner from the General Store, that he had been looking for in the first place. What he could only describe as a gothic-style mansion sat next to an open area that looked like a public park. The house had a hand-carved sign out front that read: *Francis Thistle, M.D.*

Trey shoved his fear and confusion deep down and stomped across the street to talk to Will Bainbridge.

11

The boy screamed as it tore his nose off with its teeth. It plunged its fingers into his eye sockets, causing blood to pool and run down his cheeks. He was nearly a man, but he still had the taste that it liked. The taste of youth.

The shattered face twisted as the boy shook violently, as if he could shake it off. It was as strong as the fir. It could not be stopped. The boy was naked, his clothing torn off during the chase. It planned to feast on more of him than usual. His flesh looked so good. She would allow it. She would understand. It only fed because it was her will that it did so. The Elder One demanded a sacrifice. She demanded that it feed.

The boy flailed and kicked, all while choking on the blood that covered his ruined face. It snapped one of his arms at the elbow and began to suck the marrow where the bone erupted from the skin. The boy stopped thrashing and whimpered now. He would not last long. It rolled the boy over and began to tear meat from his haunches. This had been the best meal it had eaten in a long time.

When it was done, it hoisted what was left of the boy into the air and impaled him on a tree branch. The bloodied body drooped—a marionette with broken strings. It watched for some time as the blood and viscera from the boy fell to the roots of the tree. She would be most pleased. She Who Shatters Time. This cycle was the strongest yet. The closest she had come to waking. It had done well. Only a few cycles remained.

The dreamer cried this time. It was the morning of October 16th, and they knew who it was that would be found today. The same boy who had died in the dream, even if that death had happened over a hundred years ago. They knew everyone in town, but this…this had been different. This boy was someone who thought the dreamer was safe. And now they were gone.

The others wouldn't care. They wouldn't understand. The cycle must continue. The dreamer must feed so that Kythk'uhn could return. That meant people they knew had to die. People like Chance Bainbridge.

12

Even though the "hospital" in Jackson Point was actually just the Doctor's private residence, Trey was shocked that the foyer inside felt like a real waiting room. Sure, the furnishings looked like they had been stolen from a Hammer Horror film, but that hopeless, anesthetic-filled air covered any lingering smells of dust or mothballs. What had once likely been carpeting or hardwood was covered with sterile linoleum, and all of the lights were garish fluorescent tubes.

A plump woman sat behind a window like you would expect at a normal Doctor's office. She looked at Trey with dead eyes when he entered, though her voice was far more chipper than he would have assumed.

"Welcome! How may I help you today?" she asked.

"I need to see Will Bainbridge," Trey responded, trying to hide the fear in his voice. "I uh, it was my car that he hit last night, and we need to exchange insurance information."

"Oh!" the woman covered her mouth. "You are the young man who helped keep him stable before Dr. Thistle got there. Well, follow me!"

The receptionist led Trey through an archway into a much larger room dominated by a staircase in the center. They ascended the steps to the second-floor landing. A sign with an arrow stood at the top of the stairs, mounted on an old coat rack. The sign pointed to the right above the words "Patient Wing". The woman stopped here to polish the banister with her sleeve. She pointed down the hall.

"Mr. Bainbridge is in Room 7, it's the fourth door on your left."

Trey smiled weakly at her before he shuffled down the hall. The walls were dark and foreboding up here, unlike the bright sterility of the waiting room. Lights with bare tungsten bulbs protruded every so often from sconces on the walls, and cobwebs seemed to cling in every corner where the light refused to penetrate fully. Behind it all was a faint hum, like the sound of electricity moving through failing wires.

It didn't take long to arrive outside the oak door with a "7" nailed to it. Trey hesitated at the threshold. This was insane, like everything about the last two days. What was he going to actually ask the man? *Did your son really die? Did they find him today, even though his funeral was last night? Why did you crash into my car? What is wrong with this fucking town?*

He tried to tamp down his fears and let his journalism training take over. The weird shit was secondary. Trey still had a podcast to run and a book to write. Reaching into his pocket, Trey clicked on his recorder. After two short raps on the door, he turned the knob before waiting for a reply.

Inside the room, Will Bainbridge sat propped up on a standard-looking hospital bed, which sat opposite a large wooden dresser. The curtains were drawn, filling the room with patches of inky darkness. The man slowly turned to look at Trey. His face was taut as if from pain, and he had great bags under his eyes. Even in the dim room, Trey could see the resemblance to the picture of Chance from the cemetery. Like his son, Will had a head of shaggy brown hair, though his face was much rounder than his son's.

"Mr. Bainbridge," Trey said as he sat down in a wooden chair with a plush red and gold cushion. "My name is Treyton Savage. I'm the owner of the car that you hit last night."

Will simply gave him a thousand-yard stare. Trey was so unnerved momentarily that he looked over his shoulder to make sure that no one was, in fact, standing behind him. The door to the room was shrouded in shadows, but no one had joined them.

"Mr. Bainbridge, I need to ask you some questions. I'm not from around here, as I'm sure you've noticed. I actually…" Trey paused, thinking about how best to not be insensitive. "I came to Jackson Point to find out everything I can about your son's killer. I need your help."

The man's head suddenly snapped in Trey's direction, and his eyes focused on the podcaster. He ran his tongue over his cracked lips before slowly speaking.

"You want to know about Chance?" he asked.

"Yes," Trey replied. "And what happened last night when you hit my car?"

Will looked toward the window, even though the black curtains obstructed any view of the woods beyond. When his gaze returned, he looked even more hollow than before.

"It was an accident," he whispered. "She only cut me because she thought I could trade places with Chance. That's all. I'm sorry about your car…"

Trey went cold. That explained the wound on his chest. It wasn't *from* the car accident, but the reason for it.

"She cut you? Who cut you? Your wife?"

"Gloria didn't do anything wrong," the man continued. "She just wanted our boy back. She hoped that we could trade, Chance and I. That's all."

"But Chance is dead, Mr. Bainbridge. How could that change?"

"The Rootmother sometimes gives those she's taken back. Maybe she takes them again, maybe she takes someone else. Gloria hoped she would take me..."

He looked away again, just as tears started streaming down his face. Trey noticed that Will had begun to dig his fingers into his legs. Behind him, the heart monitor began to spike.

"Who is this Rootmother?" Trey continued. "I've been here two days and I've heard her name half a dozen times."

Will turned back again, his thousand-yard stare returned.

"Two days?" Then the man threw back his head and cackled, flecks of spit tinged with blood coating his lips. "Boy, you've always been here, and you always will be. You felled the first tree here, and sealed your fate, just like the rest of us."

Trey gripped the arms of his chair and leaned forward, all veneer of professionalism dropping away.

"What the hell does that mean? Why does everyone here talk in fucking riddles about broken time and tree roots? Why was your son's funeral last night, but he was found Wednesday morning, *this* morning?"

Will stopped laughing.

"What did you say?"

"That's why I came here to talk to you! I've been losing time since I got here. It should have been Tuesday when I woke up, but it was Friday. And now this morning it's Wednesday again, the same Wednesday morning when they said they found Chance's body. Tell me what's happening?!"

Will lunged forward, causing Trey to tumble to the floor. He thought the man was trying to grab him, but instead, he simply threw himself out of bed, pulling all of his IVs and monitors loose as he did so. Trey tried to stand so that he could help the man, but he was kicked back down to the floor. The enraged patient began throwing open the drawers of the dresser opposite his bed while screaming at the top of his lungs.

"She has given us a chance! They haven't found it yet, there's still time!" Will shouted.

He began throwing the drawers of the dresser aside, causing Trey to scramble under the bed for protection. Then, just as suddenly as the madness began, it stopped. From his hiding place, Trey could only see Will's socks and the bottom of his hospital gown. He crawled back out into the open to see what the deranged man had found.

Will was holding a scalpel in his right hand. Tears were streaming down his face, but he was smiling for the first time since Trey had come to see him.

"I still have time. I must nourish the roots, and she will give us back our son."

"No!" Trey screamed, but it was too late.

Will Bainbridge gouged out both of his eyes with the scalpel before jamming it into his throat. Then, as if he were still able to see, he sprang right through the window. The shattering of the glass and Trey's cries brought a clamor of footsteps down the hall. Just as the door opened, Trey looked over the edge of the window frame. Will Bainbridge lay dead at the base of a towering pine. Multiple sets of hands wrapped around Trey's midsection and pulled him back from the window.

"Someone call the sheriff!" a voice yelled.

That was the last thing Trey heard.

13

Kevin tried to focus during early morning gym warm-ups, but his mind was awash with fear. It was Wednesday again. And while most residents of the town either hadn't noticed or didn't care that the week had moved backward, Kevin knew. He also knew that meant that there was a possibility that he would see Chance again today, dead or otherwise.

His parents were in the group that pretended nothing was happening. When they awoke to see their calendars set forward or backward days at a time from what they would have expected the night before, they simply smiled and went about their day. When Kevin mentioned it to them, they would laugh and tell him that he was mistaken.

He had been ten when he had first noticed

that time didn't behave in Jackson Point the way he was told it did in the rest of the world. His cat Mittens had been hit by a car one day, leaving nothing but a broken body on the side of the road. Kevin's father had buried Mittens in the backyard and the family held a mock funeral. Everyone had cried, but Kevin knew Mittens would be in heaven with Jesus. His grandmother told him that Mittens was nourishing the roots now. Then the next day, Mittens had been alive again. He told his parents about the miracle, but they had acted like it had only been a bad dream. Only his grandmother seemed to believe him, but she also insisted that he not talk about it. When Kevin went out to the backyard he found that Mitten's grave was still there, so he got a shovel and started to dig. Before he got to the little cardboard box that his cat should have been in, there was a screeching sound out front, and she was gone again—killed by the same car at almost the same time.

That made Kevin pay attention. Some weeks passed like normal, some had fewer days than others, and some had twice as many. Clocks and calendars kept pace, changing and showing impossible dates as if everything was working as it should. The adults all acted like it was normal to work eight straight days and then have five days off. Weekends could last for months sometimes, yet food didn't run out. Time just stopped—or rewound—or fast-forwarded. It was like Jackson Point was a VHS tape in his grandma's house, and God was playing with the remote.

Outsiders noticed the distortions the most. While they were still outsiders, that is. Ms. Moore, for example, had nearly been committed to one of the padded rooms in Dr. Thistle's basement before she got used to it. *Right around the time she started teaching*, Kevin thought. And now that Kevin had lured Trey here, he would either adapt, die, or go mad. A pang of guilt struck Kevin, but he pushed it aside. Someone had to help Chance. Someone had to stop the killings, even if they couldn't fix time.

The shrill whistle from Mr. Nelson sounded. Everyone stopped their warm-ups and gathered in a circle around the Gym Teacher. He was a large man with well-toned muscles and a shiny bald head. Today, he was wearing a navy tracksuit adorned with nothing but his bright silver whistle and his usual yellow sneakers. Mr. Nelson was the Gym Teacher, Math Teacher, and Coach of whatever athletics team the school could cobble together on any given year. He was also the only adult at the school besides Ms. Moore who treated Kevin like he meant something.

"Alright, it's a nice autumn morning," he said

with a grin. "Why don't we go for a jog around town? You all know the route, up Eichle, back across 1st, down Main, and then back here. Let's get moving! No messing around today, alright? Sylvans don't dawdle—"

"They grow!" the students answered.

Kevin fell into line behind the other joggers. He wasn't very athletic, so these morning jogs were often the low point of his day. Gym was split into two halves in the morning: the kindergarteners through 5th graders in one batch, and then everyone else in the other. That meant about thirty students were running through Jackson Point right now. Kevin simply didn't want to be at the back of them.

The group rounded the first turn from the school and started up Eichle. After a few minutes of running down the middle of the street, they passed the cemetery down the road to their right. Most of the giggling and chatter stopped. Kevin imagined that nearly everyone here had been at Chance's funeral last night.

Friday night, he thought. But it's Wednesday again. *Please, don't let him be there.*

The joggers continued on, the glum pall hanging over them all even as they passed the cemetery. They were thinking exactly what Kevin was. It had been on this jog that they had found him, the last time *this* Wednesday had come around. Kevin felt sick. He had hoped that it wouldn't happen this time, or that if it did, he would have at least forgotten that he had lived it once. Neither thing had been true. Now his only hope was that it would be different. That Chance wouldn't be there—he was just missing from school today because he was sick, or because his dad was in the hospital. *In the hospital because you are dead.*

The intersection that he was dreading arrived, where Eichle ran into 1st. The group turned to the left, none so much as looking down the road to the right where the ruins of Frederick Ansel's home lay. A scream tore through the morning, just as it had last time. The group stopped short. Hanging from a tree, with all of his limbs broken at odd angles, was the naked body of Chance Bainbridge. Most of his face had been torn off, but Kevin still knew it was him. He tried to swallow down the bile this time, but it was no use.

Kevin and a dozen others vomited in the middle of the road. The eyeless corpse of their classmate was watching them with disinterest.

14

Samantha tossed most of the homework assignments into the garbage bin under her desk. She had already graded most of these, twice. Sometimes the answers came back a little different, but ultimately it didn't matter. Her students were forced to do the same homework time and time again, and everyone around them had to pretend that nothing was wrong.

She leaned back in her chair and pulled out the thermos that she kept beneath her desk. It held coffee and whiskey in equal parts. Prior to moving to this godforsaken place, Sam hadn't even drunk a single beer in her life. Now, she was basically a functioning alcoholic just to keep herself sane. It was harder for outsiders, they told her. Those who grew up here were just used to it. Seeing the trauma that her students went through on a weekly basis, she didn't think that that was true.

The adults are all just so fucked up they can't help but go along with it, she thought.

Everyone wondered why she had moved there herself. Why, in God's name, would a young Black woman move to a small white town like this? Why would *anyone* move to Jackson Point? So far, in the last twelve years, she hadn't told a soul. So far, she hadn't found what she was looking for. And once she did, then what? *Then I'm still stuck here like everyone else.*

From what she had gleaned over the last decade-plus in this hellhole, everything bad that happened could be traced back to Frederick Ansel. That racist bastard had thought he was god's gift to the Oregon territory and forced a logging camp in a place that no one in their right mind would've stayed a week in, let alone permanently. The ground here was bad. You could feel it just walking through the place. There was a reason most pets were indoors in Jackson Point. Anything left outside went rabid or died. The trees grew back at an alarming rate, meaning nothing could truly be cleared away for new development. Everything that was already here just decayed and was rebuilt.

People could leave, of course, though not for more than a few hours. Husbands would travel to Hood River or The Dalles to buy cars and come back by nightfall looking like they'd seen a ghost. Most who tried to leave for good found themselves right back where they started. Once or twice, Sam heard about someone getting out, a wife running off while the husband negotiated at the dealership, a son who snuck away in the back of a delivery truck that came into town. Those always ended the same way: suicide.

Something kept people here, and for the last twelve years, Samantha Moore had been rooted to this spot along with all of the others. She didn't know exactly what it was that Frederick Ansel had built his timber mecca over, but she knew that it was foul. The locals called it the Rootmother, or sometimes the Green Goddess, "She Who Sleeps Beneath the Trees", but no one really knew what it was, even if Sam had her suspicions. What the people did know, what Sam had seen firsthand, was that whoever talked about the Rootmother too much ended up dead, in one way or another.

She popped her neck from side to side and looked out the window, watching as the morning gym class ran towards Eichle Street. Sam knew what was coming next. Someone or some*thing* had been killing people in the town, and now it had gotten one of her students. Rubbing her eyes, she took another swig of the spiked coffee. They would find Chance, just like they did last time this day rolled around, and then the grieving would start all over, fresh in their minds after seeing his corpse for the second time in three days. There were days when she thought death would be a mercy, for all of them. Today was one such day.

"Ms. Moore," a man said from the doorway.

She closed her thermos and spun in her chair, putting on that smile that she reserved for white folks alone.

"Mr. Abner," she said. "How can I be of service?"

Principal Clinton Abner was a thick man with a white beard that covered his jowls. If he wasn't such a pompous asshole, he would have made a great mall Santa. Still, he was the one who signed Sam's checks, so she had to kiss his ass more than most.

Clinton crossed the small classroom and ran his fingers across the blackboard, examining the chalk powder when he was done. He always did this, as if he were doing some type of white-glove inspection of a schoolroom that was built over a hundred years ago.

"I'd like you to take the day off, Samantha," he said finally, with an air of distaste.

"Take the day off?" For once, the confusion in her voice was genuine.

"Cut the crap, Samantha," Clinton said, leaning against a desk. "I know transitioning to the...way things are around here has been difficult for someone like *you*."

Sam bristled. He was rarely this open.

"Someone like me?"

"An outsider," he replied with a wicked smile. "You and I both know what the children are likely to find on their jog this morning. We need them to be able to mourn and move on, not harp on the fact that this is the second time they've seen the poor Bainbridge boy strung up. And I don't think you're capable of facilitating that."

The skin on her knuckles paled as she gripped the edge of her desk.

"And why is that?" she asked through gritted teeth. "I've worked through every other tragedy that has struck this town. I worked last Wedne— last time Chance was found. What makes today different?"

Clinton stood up and walked over to her desk, leaning across it so that his face was uncomfortably close to hers. His breath smelled like raw meat. It took all of her self-control not to slap him backward.

"What's different is that there is another outsider in town, asking questions. I don't want any trouble stirred up, and neither does the rest of the city council, so I am telling you to *go home*. I will personally finish out your duties today. Understood?"

"Understood," Sam said.

She stood and grabbed her things, walking quickly to the door. She had no desire to sit and chat with that bastard a moment longer than she had to.

"Oh, Samantha," Clinton called. "You forgot this."

Sam turned to see that he was holding up her thermos. She hoped that the lid was on tight enough that he couldn't smell the liquor. Though he had likely smelled it on her breath already.

"One more thing, my dear," he said as she took the thermos from him.

"Is there anything I should know about young Mr. Anderhoff? I saw him sitting with the outsider at the funeral last night."

Sam shook her head and walked out the door. That boy was in over his head, and she was running out of time.

15

The ride in the back of the police cruiser had been a blur. Trey spent most of the short drive sobbing and gasping for air. He had looked at hundreds of crime scene photos in his short career as a True Crime podcaster, but he had never seen someone die up close, especially in such a violent and visceral way. But it wasn't even the suicide itself that left him so rattled. It was the *why*. Will Bainbridge had believed so thoroughly that he had a chance at saving his son that he had brutally taken his own life, all to appease this so-called Rootmother. Based on the "Undead" portion of his show, Trey had done quite a bit of research into folk tales and legends from around the world. The best he could surmise about Jackson Point was that the town was engaged in the worship of some pagan deity, not unlike Leshy from Slavic myths. A crazed, town-wide delusion or belief system would explain a lot about this town—but not the broken time.

By the time they parked outside the police station, he had calmed down. Trey knew that was likely shock setting in again. Not just from the death, but from all of it. The inside of the station looked just like any other, though it was considerably smaller than any of the ones Trey had visited while cycling through the various Portland newspapers. From what he could tell, the department only really consisted of three officers and the Chief, or three deputies and the sheriff, rather.

Though that would make her an elected county official, he thought. *Which I'm sure she isn't.*

He was led to an uncomfortable chair at a desk in the back of the room. A paper cup filled with water was set in front of him, and then he was left alone for what felt like hours. Finally, the pixie-cut blonde who was the sheriff of Jackson Point sat down in front of him. Her brown and tan uniform looked freshly pressed, but Trey couldn't help but notice the dark stains across the front. Stains that still glistened from wet blood.

Trey tried to hide his nervousness. Living in

Portland through the BLM protests had left him with a well-earned distrust of police. And he had never been questioned directly before. Sheriff Tench simply looked him over for the next several minutes before she spoke.

"What are you doing here, Mr. Savage?" she asked, her voice ice.

"Uh-I assumed you wanted to ask me questions about th-the suicide," Trey mumbled.

"Don't play coy with me, jackass," she snapped. "We'll get to that if it really *was* a suicide. I want to know why you, some Portland hipster podcaster, is in my town causing trouble."

Trey took his first sip of water from the now-dissolving cup. He didn't like how this was starting out. Not at all.

"I came here to do a story on the murders," he said, finally. "I'm a journalist—yes, I have a podcast, but I also run a blog, and I planned to do a book about small-town serial killers, starting with Jackson Point."

As he said it out loud, his credentials sounded far weaker than they did in his head. He considered adding that *The Dead and the Undead* average a few million downloads per month. The look on her face told him that she wouldn't have cared. The sheriff started writing something down on her legal pad. Trey took another sip. The sounds of her pen scratching on the paper made his skin crawl.

"Where are you staying?" she asked without looking up.

"Best Boarding House," he replied, annoyance entering his voice. "But you know that already. Aren't you going to ask me about what happened to Will?"

She still didn't look up, but her pen seemed to dig deeper into the pad. Trey was sure that she would have poked through to the next page by now.

"How long have you been in town?" she asked.

He paused. He really didn't know how to answer. The sheriff finally looked up, her eyes boring a hole through him.

"I-I don't know," he stuttered. "I left Portland on Monday and got here just after midnight on Tuesday, but that wasn't yesterday, that was three days ago to me...but then again, maybe five. I don't understand what's going on."

He saw a flash of compassion behind her eyes, but then they were flint again.

"Are you a drug user, Mr. Savage?"

"No. I mean, I smoke weed sometimes, but not since I've been here. I didn't even bring my vape. What does that have to do with anything?"

"Your confusion about the length of your stay sounds like the inane ramblings of an addict," she replied.

That filled him with a rage that he had thought he had lost. He slammed his fist on the desk, spilling the last little bit of water onto the floor.

"I know you know what's going on in this town!" he shouted. "Something is fucked up with time, ever since I got here. Last night was that boy's funeral, and I saw you there. Don't tell me I didn't! And that was on a Friday. And now it's suddenly the Wednesday before, and—"

One of the deputies walked around Trey, completely unfazed by his tirade. The deputy leaned in and whispered something to the sheriff. Her face paled, and she dropped her pen. When the man was done talking to her, she stood up and cast one last wary glance down at Trey.

"We are done here, Mr. Savage," she said.

"What about Will?" he demanded.

"I have to go cut his son down from a tree for the second time this week."

With that, she stomped off, though he could tell by her body language that she regretted admitting that to him. So much for being the ramblings of an addict, he thought. Though he thought that this simply being a bad trip was likely preferable to his current reality. He was alone in the station for a few minutes before he realized that this was his first chance to see one of the bodies up close. Trey reached into his pocket and shut off his recorder before the battery died—he knew the last hour that he had recorded would either be invaluable for his book, or prove that he hadn't lost his mind—and then jumped up and ran out the door.

Thankfully, Trey hadn't sat dumbfounded for so long that he missed the sight of the squad car turning onto 1st Street. He sprinted after them, trying not to look into Dylan's to see if his car was on the rack yet. He didn't want to even think about what it would mean to be truly stuck here. No matter what any of them told him, he was going to drive out of this place as soon as he was done.

The police were taping off half of the block when he got there. A crowd was forming to stare at the desecrated corpse that hung impaled from one of the lower branches of the pine tree. Trey tried to steel his nerves for what was to come next. He knew that looking at crime scene photos on the internet would be nothing compared to being here and potentially taking some of his own.

He moved down the block parallel to the crime scene, nudging his way through onlookers who barely gave him a second glance. As he did so, he caught snippets of conversations that he tried to store in his mind for later.

"It'll stick this time, the second death always does," a woman said.

"Not always," replied a man beside her. "Remember the White girl? She died four or five times if I remember right, poor thing."

And then another person farther down asked, "Did you hear about his father? I heard he jumped right out of Thistle's today and died. Splat. Just like that. I guess he didn't want to see his boy like this twice."

"The kids found him again on their jog. I know we've got to keep things moving, but you'd think they'd at least make them run a different way just in case."

Trey's stomach churned. He hoped that didn't include Kevin. The thought of the poor kid finding his best friend like this *once* was bad enough, but twice? *Jesus Christ.* When he was finally directly across from the body, he pulled out his phone and zoomed in, taking as many pictures as he could without drawing attention to himself.

The boy's body looked like it had been savaged by wolves. His limbs were all broken, and bits of flesh were torn off here and there. From this distance, it was hard to tell for sure, but Trey knew somehow that this had been done with teeth. Worst of all was his face. Nothing remained of the smiling boy in the memorial picture at the funeral. Instead, a bloody skull with no eyes leered at him. His entire face and nose had been torn all of the way off.

Trey felt his stomach churning, but he was able to hold back from letting anything up. The smell, though, nearly did him in. From this distance, even, he could smell a mix of copper and pine, tree and blood, on the wind. It was sickly sweet. He looked at the faces of those in the crowd. None seemed even the least bit queasy. This was far too normal to them.

Finally, he gained enough courage to ask one of the people he was standing next to some questions. His fingers slipped back into his pocket and turned on the recorder before he began. The closest man next to him had a familiar shape. The man was large and seemed as much the spitting image of a lumberjack as Trey had ever seen. He was wearing a flannel shirt rolled up to expose his hair-covered forearms, and suspenders held up his jeans. That was when Trey recognized him. Mayor Tench. Cousin to the sheriff, who was right now organizing an effort to set up a ladder to cut the boy down.

"Were they all like this? Strung up, I mean?" Trey asked.

"Yes, though not all right here, of course," the mayor responded, absentmindedly.

"When did the first body show up? And did it come back like Chance?"

That got the mayor's undivided attention. The large man suddenly loomed over Trey, his breath forming small puffs in the morning air. His eyes were hard, not unlike his cousin's, but Trey had a feeling that most of that was for show.

"Mr...Savage, was it? I don't appreciate you sniffing around my town, trying to turn our private tragedies into clickbait. Think of the family of this here boy."

"The family?" Trey asked, his rage building again. "You mean Will Bainbridge, who took his own life right in front of me a little over an hour ago? Or Gloria Bainbridge, who tried to kill her husband in some vain attempt to stop this," Trey pointed an accusatory finger at the dead boy, "from happening again? Is that the family you are talking about?"

Tench took a step back, clearly not expecting Trey's outburst. Both men looked back just as the body of Chance was being lowered to the ground. Sheriff Tench saw them and began walking over.

"You watch yourself, outsider," the mayor whispered.

"You too, Mayor," Trey said.

Then he slipped into the crowd and was gone.

16

It crawled through the underbrush like an animal, uprooting ferns and snapping fallen branches in its wake. Here, deeper in the forest, away from the camp, it could commune with the Elder One better. It felt her presence in the earth and the trees, and the fallen leaves. It smelled her on the air. It wished to hold her in its embrace, to ravage her with its loins. She called out through the wind, an inhuman voice that spoke in a tongue unrecognizable to all but her servants. The language of the stars.

Its massive fingers dug into the earth, waiting for more of her to come. Soon, roots began to emerge from the soil, pushing up like grubs after the rain. Once these roots would have been less than shoots, no larger than a human hair. Now, this far into the cycle, they were each the size of a man's wrist. The roots wrapped around it and pulled it down, deeper and deeper into the earth, until it was trapped in her embrace.

This is where it had been made, in the time before time. This is where it would be made again, after the last cycle, when the stars were right, the Elder One could wake. It opened its mouth and tasted her flesh this time. The flesh of bark and sap and root, and soil. Flesh that gave it strength and nourished its body more than any human sacrifice. The flesh of a Goddess.

Then she entered it, and it was filled with ecstasy. Her tendrils pierced it and throbbed inside, filling it with her blood. It would be stronger after this. It would be time for this cycle to come to a close. *Soon.* But there was still much feeding to be done.

When it awoke above ground, the crickets had begun their nightly noises. Ahead, a wagon made its way up the muddy road, bringing with it a family of one of the loggers. Inside the wagon, a babe cried, wailing for milk from its mother. Though it had just received sustenance from the Elder One, it suddenly hungered again.

❦

The dreamer awoke screaming this time, flailing as they fell out of bed. Why was the dream like this? Why now? It was still early in the cycle. It wasn't time for things to end. That was not what they had said. That was not what they had promised. It was only October 10th. Only four bodies had been found yet. *And today, a fifth,* they thought.

Yet they were already dreaming—remembering the end of the cycle. Why? All they knew was that the end was coming. The end that hopefully meant she would wake.

17

Trey stormed into the library, still fired up from his confrontation with the mayor. After the veiled threats the two men had thrown at each other, Trey felt like he should have been more afraid than he was. Some of that had been an act, the firebrand reporter rearing its imaginary head to protect the frightened man with impostor syndrome. But some of it had been true. There was a rot in this town that was beginning to piss him off, and he intended to get to the bottom of it.

Slipping past the front desk without so much as checking to see if any of the librarians were in, he raced up the spiral stairs to the top floor where the Local History section was. Once there, he scooped up an armful of books, including a new one: *Paganism & Pioneers*, which had not been on the shelf the previous day. Taking his armful of research, he picked out a reading room, threw the books onto a table, and set to work, all while trying not to imagine Becca pressed up against the wall.

First, he started with the Ansel biography, flipping toward the end where he could find out more about the man's death—and why it might have coincided with the same calendar date that Trey arrived in Jackson Point. After thumbing through the last few chapters, he realized that this book also glossed over the death of the man, though not as much as *Jackson Point: A History of Blood and Sap* did. He chewed his lip as he scanned the pages, looking for anything worth taking a picture of.

Finally, he found something of interest:

> *On the night of October 14th, an otherwise sleepy Thursday marked by a period of heavy rain, disaster struck the town of Jackson Point. Frederick Ansel was found dead in his manor, amidst a roiling inferno that was only just quenched by the storm. The exact details surrounding Ansel's death remain a mystery to this day, but rumors of the time were often recorded in more salacious news sources or even in occult circles of the period.*
>
> *One such account says that Ansel was slain by*

a long-lost son who had come to claim his inheritance, but had been rebuffed, slitting his father's throat and burning the manor in recompense. This can be easily disputed, however, as there has never been any substantiated record of Ansel having any offspring at all. In fact, it was recorded that the man may have had a genital disfigurement that would have prevented copulation at all (which I did not cover in his early years because this itself is unsubstantiated).

The next popular tale is that of the 'Green Goddess' and her cult. The 'Green Goddess' was supposedly a being out of local Indian myth, though there is little evidence to back that up. Neither the Columbia Indians nor the Chinook tribes of the area make any reference to this being, though they are known to have avoided the area where the camp was eventually founded. In any case, as this theory goes, there was a cult to this malefic being who lived under the forest there, and Ansel became one of many victims sacrificed to appease her appetite. It is this author's opinion that it is far more likely that Ansel was killed by a jealous camp worker, such as Victor Tench, who purchased the mill shortly after Ansel's death.

Finally, the most outlandish theory of all: that Frederick Ansel had become obsessed with this 'Green Goddess' himself, and that he had begun making sacrifices in the woods to ensure that his *mill operation would continue to bring him untold wealth. At some point, however, Ansel reneged on his pact with this deity and was killed in response— possibly even by suicide in some accounts. Of course, this is easy to see as an alteration of 'deals with the devil' type stories that were common at the time to explain how certain early capitalists came into power. It should be noted, however, that there was a string of grisly murders noted around the camp at this time that went unsolved. It would be hard to attribute these to Ansel, though, as the older man certainly couldn't have 'ripped grown men limb from limb' or even 'tore flesh from bone with monstrous teeth'. If you recall from Chapter 13, Ansel had had a set of false teeth since his thirty-second birthday. (For more information on this 'Green Goddess' and other pagan entities suppos-edly encountered by the founders of the Oregon ter-ritory, refer to* Paganism & Pioneers *by J. B. French.)*

For more reading about what happened after Ansel's untimely demise, I recommend that you read the stellar work, Jackson Point: A History of Blood and Sap *by John MacLeod.*

Trey read the passage a second time before he took the required pictures. He felt his blood run cold. While the author of this biography, a clearly pompous ass named Michael Tener, didn't take any stock in the rumors of Ansel's demise, Trey couldn't help but see the parallels to what was going on now. And this 'Green Goddess' was very likely another name for the Rootmother.

Has this really happened before? he thought.

Belatedly, he realized that he had *Paganism & Pioneers* sitting on the table beside him. He quickly flipped through the index and ran his finger down until he found Green Goddess. Turning to the first page where she was mentioned, he was greeted with a startling image.

Taking up the entire page facing the chapter about this entity was a woodcut of a tree with roots that protruded from the ground, impaling all manner of man and beast. Below the wood-cutting, it read: *Artist Unknown, Woodcut circa 1815.* From what he remembered, that was some fifteen years before Jackson Point was even founded. That meant that these "rumors" around Ansel's death had origins at least eighty-two years before the man's death. There was more there than just the run-of-the-mill deals with the devil bullshit. Unfortunately, the chapter about this entity wasn't very long, but Trey made sure to take photos of the most relevant section:

Early settlers to the region were said to have stayed far away from the grove of the Green Goddess, for she demanded a sacrifice of those who took shelter on her land. Her influence was said to extend from the area around Wahtum Lake for several miles. Because of this, some early sources refer to her as a water goddess, though this seems to have fallen out of favor by the time of Fort Vancouver.

When the area was finally settled, some complained of what we would now call 'time-blindness'. Many early settlers to the region claimed to have lost days or weeks at a time, and others said that they relived the same day more than once. Many of these claims have been attributed to an outbreak of rabies among the new communities.

Other names for the Green Goddess included: the Elder One, Queen of the Mountain Mist, Rootmother, the Time-Shattered, She Who Sleeps Beneath the Trees, and for those who refused to take heed to local superstitions: the Bitch of the Bark. While unsubstantiated, it does seem that certain older esoteric texts mention the name Khythk'uhn when referring to a being that has many similarities with the Green Goddess.

Today, there isn't much in the way of continued belief in the Green Goddess besides a few local phrases that those in the area would find quaint. However, there is an odd outcropping of stones in the town of Jackson Point referred to as 'The Elder One's Crown,' which was at one time believed to have been a crown sticking off of the Green God-

dess's head from where she slumbered beneath the region.

Trey sat back in his chair, dumbfounded. If he hadn't experienced it himself, he wouldn't have believed half of what he had read. But now? How could he discount all of the coincidences? Everything was clicking into place with his own experience, and that wasn't a comforting thought. What if this Green Goddess, this Root-mother, was real? Twenty-four hours ago, he would have felt crazy even thinking that, but now? The light overhead flickered for a moment, and he jumped, knocking both his chair and the book from the table.

When he bent down to pick the book up, he found a scrap of paper that had fallen out. Perhaps someone had been using it as a bookmark? When he picked up the paper, he saw a phone number was scrawled on one side. He considered leaving the number in the book but thought better of it and shoved it into his pocket. Gathering up the books, Trey left the room and returned them to the shelves, making sure that no one saw him do so.

He quickly left the library and returned to the Best Boarding House. Now there was nothing he could do but wait, either for Kevin to stop by after school, or for the owner of this number to answer the phone, which he guessed wouldn't happen until after five. With nothing but time, he settled in and began transcribing what his recorder had picked up throughout the day.

18

The phone rang through again. There was no voicemail set up, and Trey was annoyed enough that he was beginning to lose his nerve. His cellphone still didn't work, so he had to stand downstairs in the living room dialing. with Mrs. Best not ten feet away. Thankfully, the old woman was busy reading a battered V.C. Andrews book and seemed completely disinterested in what Trey was doing.

Third time's the charm, I guess, he thought as he dialed the number again.

This time it was answered on the third ring by a woman clearly out of breath from racing to the phone.

"H-hello?" she stammered.

Trey thought that her voice was familiar, but he tried to push that from his mind.

"This is Trey Savage," he said. "I found your number in a book while I was researching at the library today."

The other end of the phone was so quiet that Trey was afraid it had gone dead. Finally, the woman started speaking.

"You need to come to my place now. I'm in unit 18, toward the back of Fallen Lilly Trailer Park. Come right now."

Then she hung up. Trey stood there dumbfounded, staring at the phone. The sun was just starting to move behind the trees outside. If he moved quickly, he could probably make it there before it got dark. He ran back to his room and threw his computer and all of his notes into his backpack, and ran down the stairs two at a time. He felt silly as he called out to Mrs. Best.

"If Kevin stops by, tell him I'll catch up with him tomorrow!"

The old woman simply waved dismissively in response. Once outside the door, Trey nearly ran directly into Dylan, who was about to knock. Trey's SUV was sitting back in its parking spot, its rear end still smashed in.

"She'll drive," Dylan said. "But you'll need a body shop to make her pretty again. I don't do that."

"Thanks," Trey said, taking the keys. "What

do I owe you? I haven't called my insurance yet, to be honest."

Dylan looked at him like he had sprouted another head.

"It was taken care of by Gloria Bainbridge already."

With that, he turned around and started walking back toward his shop. Trey smiled at his good fortune and hopped into his car. It fired right up, just like Dylan had said. Carefully backing out of the spot, Trey looped around Main Street and headed up to 3rd. If he remembered correctly, the trailer park was just across from the General Store.

A minute later and he was proven correct. He pulled into the gravel drive that wound its way through the mostly dilapidated trailers until he reached a faded pink one that had an 18 emblazoned on a stake at the end of the driveway. He pulled in behind the old white sedan and cut the engine. He still had no idea what he was walking into, even though he swore that he could recognize the voice.

After a few deep breaths, he hopped up the rotting stairs and knocked on the door. Becca answered, and Trey took a reflexive step backward in shock. She wasn't wearing her pleated skirt and blouse this time, but an oversized t-shirt and a pair of men's underwear. He swallowed and tried not to look her over.

"Becca, right?" he asked, pushing his dream from his mind.

"Get in before somebody sees you," she said as she pulled him inside.

Inside her trailer was a mess, with clothing and empty take-out boxes strewn everywhere. He tried not to stare, but the state of her home was at odds with the woman that he had met in the library previously. She seemed to have caught the look on his face.

"Look, if you want to judge me you can get the fuck out," she said, her eyes filled with fury.

Trey raised his hands.

"No, no judgment. You should see my place. I just didn't expect it to be you on the other end of the phone."

She relaxed at that and made space for him on the couch. She sat on the floor across from him. He couldn't help but notice that she wasn't wearing a bra. Suddenly, he felt very warm. After a few minutes of awkward silence, he spoke.

"So...you knew I would be the one to find your number?"

"I hoped as much," she said, taking a sip of coffee from an old, cracked mug. "Look, I know I came off strong in the library, but it isn't safe there, or anywhere in the open in this town."

"I've gathered that," Trey said distantly. He couldn't help but picture Will Bainbridge gouging his eyes with the scalpel.

"Today I heard that you were a journalist, and it all started to come together."

"Podcaster," Trey corrected. For some reason, he didn't feel like over-representing himself with her. If that affected her opinion of him, she didn't show it.

"I imagine that you're here because of the murders?" she asked.

"I am. I was—am planning on writing a book, and a local listener keyed me in on the possibility of a serial killer in Jackson Point. So, here I am..."

"And what is your impression of our little hamlet so far?" A wicked smile crossed her face. He tried not to think about the blood.

"It's...pretty fucked," he admitted. "I know that everyone in town believes in some kind of forest goddess, I know that time doesn't work right here, and I know that whatever is happening now has happened at least once before, back when Frederick Ansel died."

Becca nodded as he spoke, sipping on her coffee. She didn't speak again for some time after he finished. He finally had to look at his hands to stop staring at her.

"It takes a long time for us kids to figure out

what the adults already know in this town. Most refuse to talk about it. About *her*. The Root-mother. They just accept her, like the way time works here, as a fact of life. We can't escape it, so why fight it? Right? Well, let me tell you about when I decided that was bullshit, and I needed to find a way to figure out what this bitch is and put a stop to her."

Trey nodded and pulled out his recorder. He looked for her approval, and she gave him a curt nod before continuing.

"When I was younger, my family had a house out on Davis Road. You'll find that most folks actually live outside of the town itself, but they are under *her* influence all the same. Anyways, we had a house out there, almost like a home-stead. My dad worked at Tench Mill, and my mom stayed home and took care of chickens and goats, and…my sister.

"I was sixteen when this happened, see? I was just starting to drive, and my dad had gone and gotten me that beater you saw in the driveway for my birthday. So, of course, I was driving up and down Davis, into town to grab a burger from Happy's Burgers or stopping to meet some friends at Eaton's. You know how it is.

"One night, a few weeks after I got my car, I was out later than I should have been. My par-ents didn't talk about *her*, too much. They didn't want to scare us. But my mom always said to watch where you dig after dark. Anyway, I was out in town past dark, fooling around with some boy. When we were done, I drove home…I didn't get halfway there, and I saw the night sky was orange. Something had started a fire and burned down the whole house with everyone inside.

By the time I got there, the volunteer fire department was inside looking for survivors. They found my parents dead, but no sign of Jenni, my…my little sister. Jenni and I were never super close, too big of an age gap, you know? But she made me this mug for my birthday."

Becca started to cry. Trey moved to comfort her, but she shooed him away.

"Well, as soon as I got there and saw my parents laid out under some tarps, I fell to my knees and started crying. That's when Jenni came running. Nobody knew where she had been hiding, but somehow she had survived long enough to hear me. So out comes this little girl—I think she was eight, running towards me screaming 'cause she was on fire. Her hair was gone, and her skin was melting off, and she still came running to her big sister to save her.

"She was dead by the time she got to me."

"Oh my god," Trey said dumbly. "Becca, I'm so sorry."

"That ain't the worst of it," she whispered.

"I'm sure time has fucked with you since you've been here? It's different for all of us, but I heard they cut the Bainbridge boy down again today, so that means a few days have repeated for you."

Trey nodded. "I met you on Friday. Yesterday, I think? And now it's Wednesday."

Becca sighed and rubbed her temples.

"That's just how it is here. Sometimes a week will go by normally, or a month, and sometimes a day will repeat over and over until you go crazy. Sometimes that means two things that couldn't have both happened, happened. That's what happened with Jenni.

"The next day, my house was still burnt down —I was staying in town with friends. My parents were still dead, but Jenni, she just woke up next to me like nothing had happened. Except she remembered burning and dying. It scared her so much that she wouldn't stop crying all day. When my friend's parents tried to explain to her what happened—as if you could explain *that* to an eight-year-old, she got scared and ran off.

"We found her a few hours later, dead under some trees. Looked like she tripped on a root and split her head open. I was left alone, again, and my grief started over. Then the next day the same thing happened, 'cept Jenni remembered both times she died. That afternoon, she was hit by a car. Then it was drowning. On the fifth day, she swallowed some rat poison to escape the memories. That's when she was finally gone."

Trey sat in silence, looking at the woman crying in front of him. Her t-shirt had a small brown flower blossoming on it from where she clutched the coffee cup to her chest. He felt sick to his stomach again, and he didn't know what to do or say. Finally, he flicked the recorder off and threw it in his bag.

"What were you hoping I could do, Becca?"

"I was hoping you could help me figure out what causes this and stop it. Or at least stop these killings before more people get hurt."

"What about the sheriff?" he asked.

"Tench? That bitch isn't gonna do anything. She got her criminal justice degree online for Chrissakes. The only reason she has the job is because her family owns the mill, and her cousin is the mayor. No, this is something you and I have to do."

"And how do you know that?"

"Because of that book. You found my number, for starters," she said, standing. "I found it in the returns today, only nobody has ever checked it out. And when I went to put my number in it, it was already there. That means I planned to get in touch with you once before, and today I did it again. That means something."

Trey felt his face go flush. Whatever courage

he had mustered earlier in the day was evaporating, and quickly.

"Look, Becca," he said, standing. "I'm just a podcaster. I saw a man kill himself today, right in front of me, and then I saw his son impaled on a tree with his fucking face chewed off, okay? I am not equipped to handle this. I'm gonna get the hell out of here and see if I can send help. I've got enough recordings to at least get the state police, or hell, even the FBI to come into town."

Becca was shaking her head.

"It's too late, Trey," she whispered. "She has you already. You can't leave, not until this is over. If you want to be pissed about that, blame your listener who lured you in, but you're a resident of Jackson Point now—until you nourish the roots."

Trey walked past her and patted her awkwardly on the shoulder.

"I *will* get out of here, and I will send help."

"I dreamed about you!" she called out.

He stopped in the doorway for a moment but didn't respond.

19

The rain had started again, for the first time since Trey had checked into the boarding house. He rolled through the last stop sign and left Jackson Point behind. All thoughts of following this case to its conclusion had left his mind. He was too close to the "undead" part of his show—the part he had never put much stock in, until now. If he had been in over his head with a serial killer in a small town, he was doubly so with a primordial deity distorting reality.

Now I sound like them, he thought.

He white-knuckled the first part of the drive, refusing to slow to a safe speed. He needed to get far away from this place as quickly as possible. Even with his desire to be done with this town, Trey couldn't stop thinking about Becca and the story she had told him. A few days ago, he would have thought she was delusional and needed some psychiatric help. But after the last twenty-four hours, he knew that every word she had told him was somehow true, even if it seemed impossible.

While he hadn't been there himself, the way Becca had told the story painted a picture in Trey's mind that he couldn't shake. A little girl on fire, running toward her sister for a final embrace. The pain and confusion she must have felt in the following days—enough to cause an eight-year-old to drink rat poison. Why did the Rootmother do this to the people of this town? What did this *thing* gain from all of this suffering?

Trey rounded a corner so quickly that he fishtailed, sending a stream of water halfway up the trees on the side of the road. Still, he didn't slow down. It was as if Jackson Point was a singularity pulling him back in, and the only way to escape was to travel faster than light.

Khythk'uhn.

The strange name from the book filled his mind, and he didn't know why. When he had read it, it seemed like nonsense. But now, it was as if the guttural inhuman sounds that it would take to say this name were a native tongue to him.

"Khythk'uhn," Trey said aloud. "Khythk'uhn."

Suddenly, a large shape darted out in front of him. Trey swerved hard to the right, losing control of his vehicle in the process. In moments, he was spiraling in circles, the water from the road flying up in all directions like a cyclone. Then there was a deafening thump, and the spinning stopped. Trey blacked out when his head struck his steering wheel.

Trey awoke from the blaring of his horn. His eyes were stinging from something that was running down his face. He wiped them off with the back of his hand and saw that it was covered in blood. Gingerly, he touched his forehead and felt a sizable gash from the impact.

What did I hit? He wondered.

The rain was coming down even harder now, leaving everything beyond his headlights a wall of sparkling gray and black. The pain in his head finally caught up with him, causing him to feel sick. That's when he realized that he had lost his glasses. Fumbling around by his feet, Trey felt the edge of his frames and put them on. The left lens was cracked, but it would do for now.

He hoped that whatever he had swerved to avoid was grateful. It seemed likely that his car would have to be totaled after all. Trying to ignore the signs of a concussion, the beleaguered podcaster climbed out of his car to assess the damage. His front bumper and part of his hood were caved in at a point, almost like they had folded around something hard. He popped the hood and stared at the parts underneath that he didn't understand until being soaked by the rain was no longer appealing. As far as he could tell, he could still drive to get help.

After forcing the hood to close again, Trey looked around one final time to see what he had run into. The area here looked familiar—he was stopped at the Y on a fork. That meant he had made it just ten miles out of town. Thankfully, it also meant that the Rootmother was letting him leave. It seemed that at least part of the fears of the townfolk were unfounded then.

Trey crouched down to look under the car in one final attempt to see what he had hit. Directly under the damage was the base of the road sign that had been missing on his drive in. That couldn't have been it. He swallowed and looked down to the side of the road where it had been before. Sure enough, he could see the metallic post sticking out from between the brush. There was a sudden sinking feeling in his stomach. The sign had been missing on his way into town because someone had run into it. Because he had run into it.

"No. No no no no no," he kept repeating to himself.

Sopping wet, he clambered back into his car and stared at his now shaking hands. There was only one thing to do, but he wasn't sure he was brave enough to do it. The rain continued to hammer his windshield until bits of ice started to intermix with the water. *Sleet, just like the first night.* Still shaking, Trey pulled his phone out of his pocket and looked at the date: October 14th.

He rolled down his window and threw his phone onto the ground, then stepped on the gas and launched himself down the road toward Cascade Locks. Even after everything, he couldn't believe it. *This* couldn't be happening. It couldn't be that first night again. It couldn't. He felt the pedal touch the floor, but he refused to slow down. There was only one way to get away from this place, and that was forward.

Minutes seemed to drag like hours in the pouring rain and sleet. The black trees were smudges at the edges of his vision. Nothing was in focus but the twinkling of his headlights, the sheets of gray in front of him. If the road curved, he didn't notice. There were no other cars, no dark shapes in his path. Just an unending highway and the trees that surrounded it.

It was the first night again. The night this madness had begun. He was trapped in a loop, and he knew that no matter what he did differently this time, it would play out the same, like some fucked up *Groundhog Day*. His only hope lay ahead, in Cascade Locks; he just had to get there.

"Khyth'uhn," he whispered.

The rain began to slow, and faint lights flickered ahead between the thinning trees. He'd made it. Maybe even that same kid would be at the gas station. After seeing Trey in different clothes and with a destroyed car just hours after seeing him previously, he'd have to believe Trey's story. He'd have to. The trees gave way, and he saw the first buildings in the darkness and finally slowed down. Most were houses, but to his right, he saw what looked like a drive-through.

Did Cascade Locks look like this? he thought.

Even though it wasn't how he'd remembered it, this certainly wasn't the entrance to Jackson Point. He'd done it. He'd escaped. He noticed a sign to the left, facing into the town. Trey screeched to a stop just ahead of the sign so that he could read it by looking over his shoulder.

Jackson Rd, Wahtum Lake 3 Miles.

Trey threw back his head and laughed. It

wasn't his laugh, but one that he had heard before. The same crazed laugh that had come out of Will Bainbridge just before his suicide. They were right. All of them. Becca and Kevin, and every other nutjob in this town. Now that he was stuck here, there was no escape. No escape but one.

He undid his seatbelt and sped through Jackson Point, blasting past every stop sign without so much as slowing. Swinging wide to the right, he turned onto 1st Street and angled directly for Chance Bainbridge's tree. The engine roared under the strain as the needle on his tachometer flitted up to the red line.

The SUV slammed into the tree at nearly 90 miles per hour. It folded in on itself like an accordion, and Trey was thrown through the windshield directly into the tree. A branch, grown completely at random over decades, happened to be at just the right place to tear his head from his shoulders. The podcaster's corpse slumped against the tree and car, still twitching for several minutes.

No one came to check on the noise that night, leaving Treyton alone with nothing but the trees.

20

"Two medium Happys please, each with a Diet Coke," the woman said through Kevin's headset. "Gotta watch those calories, ya know?"

"Two medium Happys and two Diet Cokes coming right up," he repeated robotically.

Flipping the headset off, he shouted the order to Molly and Omar. They responded with a much of shrugs and grunts. None of the teens liked working at Happy's Burgers on school nights, but that was one of the few ways they could get any spending money in this town at all. Most of them would end up working at the mill in a year or two anyway.

When the order was done, Kevin went to the window and handed the woman her order. She smiled at him in that condescending way that adults often do. He knew exactly what was coming next.

"You look awfully depressed to be working at a place called Happy's," she chuckled.

Kevin resisted the urge to roll his eyes.

"The irony isn't lost on me, ma'am," he said with a forced smile.

The woman waved and drove off into the night. Normally, the general wisdom in Jackson Point was to be inside after dark or to stay together in groups. Of course that didn't stop people from driving to get shitty burgers, or from forcing their kids to "learn the value of a hard day's work." At least his mom or dad would be over at close to pick him up, so that he didn't have to walk home alone.

"I'm taking a smoke break," he called to others, tossing his headset on the counter.

He walked out back to the dumpsters where the younger staff hid a communal pack of cigarettes. Kevin didn't particularly enjoy smoking, but it was about the only way to get a break that didn't get you called a pussy by your coworkers, so he inhaled the acrid poison and popped an earbud in. Something about Trey's podcast held the answer; he knew it. One of those other cases Trey had covered in the past held some clue that would help the two of them put a stop to this. He knew that he had been right about the Rootmother taking control of the killer, and he knew that he was right about this, too.

A car shot down the road—so fast that Kevin didn't get that good of a look at it. Something about it made him uneasy, though. For a moment, he thought it could have been Trey's car, but he shoved that possibility aside. Trey wouldn't have gone to Wahtum Lake at this hour. None of the bodies had been found there, at least not this bunch.

A year or two ago, something had dragged some fishermen down into the lake. Nobody was sure what had done it, but the lake was off-limits to swimmers for several months. People always went missing or died in strange ways around Jackson Point. Sometimes they stayed dead, sometimes they didn't. But it wasn't often that they ended up displayed on trees around the town.

The next drag was long and left him sputtering for a solid minute afterward. He cued up the same episode as before and listened to the various details of the murders that he could practically recite verbatim. One of these details would jump out at him tonight, and then in the morning, he would skip school and find Trey again. They could stop this. They had to. He didn't want to see Chance in that tree again, or anybody else.

Come on, he thought. *What am I missing?*

It was the part about Kenneth Knox again. The man who had eaten multiple young girls before he had been caught. Still, nothing stuck out to Kevin, even as the cigarette shrank to the filter and he was inhaling ash. The butt spun end over end into the storm drain. Kevin watched it go, knowing that it was time for him to go back inside, defeated for the moment.

Then the epiphany came.

Why would I think this, the skeptic that I usually am? Consider this last detail about the Knox case: at each crime scene, these words were written in the victims' blood: We Eat Our Children, Just As They Ate Theirs.

Kevin froze. He replayed the passage again—twice. He hadn't figured it all out, but this was a start. He thought he knew why this was happening and how to make it stop. The rest of his shift went by without incident, and he went home with his dad, smiling the entire way.

I'm coming for you, bitch, he thought.

21

S am sat alone on the floor of her house, poring over a book on theoretical mathematics. She had actually been a math major in college and had only taken history as a minor. When she arrived in Jackson Point, they had been looking for a history teacher, and even with a slight history education under her belt, she had practically been overqualified. But math was her real passion. That was part of what had brought her here.

This particular book focused on four-dimensional space, the mathematical concept of another plane of reality that humans could not interact with or hardly even conceptualize with our perception being limited to three dimensions. While the idea had become the cornerstone of much of modern physics and mathematics, it was still gibberish to the average person. Sam wasn't interested in how 4D space influenced geometry or other fields of mathematics, but how it could influence time.

When she was in college, she did a research paper on the concept of four-dimensional beings. Once the work of science fiction, this was becoming an idea that was gaining some traction in the field. Sam postulated that four-dimensional beings could live right on top of us, but that we couldn't perceive them any more than a stick figure in a sketchbook could interact with us if it had been a living thing. These "higher beings" would likely be able to view us in the same way that we viewed two-dimensional objects, and they possibly interacted with our three-dimensional space without our knowledge. She compared it to these beings casting three-dimensional shadows into our world.

While lauded, her line of research never quite found the funding. Then everything for her had changed, and she uprooted her life to move to Jackson Point, a place that she had been afraid of since she was a little girl.

While everything that happened here was connected to the Rootmother, Sam didn't think that she was interacting with the people of this town directly. It was her shadows, her creations, that had influenced this patch of woods since before the first amphibian crawled from the ocean. Little good that understanding did for her. She could no more interact with or even drive off a fourth-dimensional being than Kevin Anderhoff's doodles could do to her.

She sighed and closed the book, scattering her notes in the process. She had been over this time and time again. The most she gleaned from any of these books was theories about how one could perceive a higher-dimensional being, but that was as far as it went. Sam didn't want to perceive the Rootmother, she wanted to kick her ass. And deep down, she knew that if any of them ever truly perceived a fourth-dimensional being, their minds likely wouldn't survive.

It would be like angels in the Old Testament, she thought. *Except this one won't be saying "Be not afraid."*

Her doorbell rang, causing her to jump. She cleaned up her mess of papers and grabbed the revolver from the end table by the door. Sliding it into the waistband at the back of her yoga pants, she cracked the door, leaving the chain at the top latched. You could never be too careful, especially in Jackson Point.

"Sam," Gideon Nelson said. "Can I come in?"

"Gid," Sam replied, letting out a long breath. "You scared me. It's late. Hold on."

She closed the door and slid her revolver back into the drawer, then undid the chain and let Gideon in. Although he was imposing size-wise, he had a soft face, and she knew that he cared for the kids more than most. The last few weeks had been hard on him, especially. Gideon followed her back into the front room, where he seated himself in her recliner and she sat on the couch. His face looked much more haggard than usual.

"It's getting worse," he whispered.

Her skin began to prickle as the large man shifted uncomfortably in the chair. He wouldn't make eye contact with her.

"What's getting worse?" she asked.

"Jackson Point. All of it. The dead folks...the dead *kids*." Sam felt that last word was laced with venom. "I came to check on you this afternoon and found Clinton in your class. He told me that he sent you home."

Sam could tell that her face had soured. She had forgotten to keep her guard up. It was too late for this shit.

"He did. The prick said that he didn't trust me around the kids today, not with *another* out-sider in town. Jesus, Gideon, I've been here for twelve years, and I've taught at the school for most of those!"

"I know—I know," he said, whispering again. "I've heard that the council is tightening the reins. Tench might get pushed out. Everyone is on edge."

"Why?" Sam asked, clenching her fists. "Frankly, this is business as usual for Jackson Point. People get killed here all of the time. It's amazing this place hasn't run out of bodies for the meat grinder. What's so goddamn different this time?"

"It just is," Gideon said, his eyes growing cold. "Listen, I came by because I want you to be safe. Things will get worse before they get better, trust me. This isn't the first time this has happened, but hopefully, it will be the last. You need to take care, maybe even take a leave of absence from the school."

She felt her blood pressure rising.

"And just how do you think that would look? Huh? They'd see an outsider, since that's still what I am to you people, stepping back to help this…this podcaster or whatever he is, and then what? I'd be out on the street. You don't think Clinton is looking for any reason to get rid of the one Black woman at the school?"

Gideon seemed to shrink away from her, sucking his bulk down into the chair.

"I'll talk to Clinton, I'll make sure you keep your job. Hell, I'll cover your classes. Please, just think about what I said."

Sam nodded silently as he stood up to go.

"We've missed you at church," he added.

"I haven't felt up to it," she replied. "Maybe Sunday."

"Shepherd Cabot would love that. He's been helping all of us adjust to these hard times."

The preacher's name made her skin crawl. There was something off about that man that she couldn't put her finger on.

"Gideon," she began, trying to come up with the right words. "Do you have any idea who's doing this? You said it's happened before…"

Gideon hesitated a moment, his face softening, then his eyes were flint once more.

"I have an idea, but I don't want to say until I'm sure."

Before he made it to the door, she grabbed him by the hand.

"Is that really it? You came by to ask me to leave work and come back to church? You used to be here every other day…"

"I haven't been sleeping well," he muttered. "I can't stop thinking about the kids finding Chance twice. And I'm the one who sent them running that way—"

Sam pulled his arm, spinning him around. He

was so much taller than her, just how she liked. She pulled him down by the collar and kissed him. His hands dropped to her hips, and he lifted her, sitting her on the end table.

"Stay. One night, for me," she moaned as his hands cupped under her shirt.

"Yes," he breathed in her ear.

22

Becca hadn't stopped pacing her front room since Trey had left. She didn't know what to do now. He wasn't going to make it out of that, she was sure. But was he going to help? And if not him, then who else? As far as she knew, there was no one she could trust in this town. All of her friendships were surface-level at best; she could never truly let someone in who could just accept what had happened to Jenni as "normal".

There were outsiders, of course. People like Samantha Moore, who hadn't been born here, and as such weren't as conditioned as the others. But most of them, Moore included, went along with the flow to not stick out and draw the ire of either the Rootmother or the city council. If Trey didn't come back to her, then she might just give up.

She picked up her mug and washed it out, leaving it on the rack to dry. Once that was done, she looked around at the state of her home and sighed. Maybe she had just scared him away.

Hipster douche, she thought.

Then she started cleaning. Every old box of take-out and empty bottle of soda was rounded up and set on the porch in bags—no matter how motivated she was, she wasn't about to walk to the dumpsters in the dark. She swept, she mopped, she shined the counters, then she pulled the old vacuum out of the closet and threw the breaker, turning it on. Once that was sorted, she got the piece of crap going and finished the front room. After that, she moved on to the bathroom and finally the bedroom, making her bed...just in case he came back that night and was too scared to go back to the boarding house. *I should have warned him about them.*

It wasn't a coincidence that they owned the only place in town where an outsider could stay and the only real estate office. Jackson Point reeling people in was good business for the Best family, no matter how caring and welcoming they seemed.

When everything was done, she sat back on her couch and sucked down as much weed as she could from her vape pen. Depending on what day it was tomorrow, she was planning on taking a closer look at Evelyn's office. Something in there had to have more information about what was really happening. What they allowed out on the shelves only scratched the surface, she was sure of it. Evelyn McReedy was a member of the city council, and something about *that* had started to bother her.

Any one of them could be doing this, she thought. *Or all of them.*

Goddammit, she needed Trey to get his dumb ass back here. If he hadn't run off half-cocked, they could have come up with a plan. Instead, she was left with weed and her vibrator for the night.

Eventually, she got tired of waiting, and she passed out on top of her sheets. Becca's last thought was that she hoped her pad would be enough that night. She didn't have enough money to do the laundry yet.

❧

She woke up early for once, her mind energized for the day. Trey had never come back, which could have meant nothing, or meant that something terrible had happened. Either way, she needed to see what day it was to know if she even worked today. The calendar had jumped ahead to the 19th, which meant that it was Saturday.

That's good, she thought.

Becca's normal days off were Sunday-Monday, and right now she needed to be in the library. Even though time had jumped forward three days, she felt more refreshed than normal. She took a hot shower and actually had time to sip her coffee rather than let it go to waste on the countertop. Then she got dressed and walked to work, showing up thirty minutes early.

Herman was nowhere to be found, though the library was already unlocked, which meant he was probably taking his morning shit. Becca clocked in and grabbed the book cart to start returns. Since it was Saturday, Evelyn wouldn't be in today—unless of course, she showed up to glare at Becca from the back of the room during storytime.

She made her rounds quickly, keeping a watchful eye for Herman. After a few fake turns around the front shelves in the children's section, she watched as Herman went back to standing behind the counter. He still hadn't noticed her, which was for the best. She wheeled the squeaky cart towards Evelyn's office, making sure to take a circuitous route in case her co-worker decided to get off his ass and look for her. Once she was next to it, she gave one final look over her shoulder and used her keys to unlock the door.

When Evelyn took over the Rare Book Room as her office, she had never changed the locks from the one that worked with the master key. Her mistake.

Becca let herself inside and closed the door quietly behind her. She didn't turn on the lights and instead was forced to rely on what little bit came through from the rest of the library. She looked at the shelves that line the square room, taking mental notes of all of the titles that could be of interest later on. So far, she couldn't make out anything specific about the town or Rootmother yet, though.

A loud clang outside made her look up. Nothing was out of place. Herman must have still been at the desk. She crouched all the same and worked her way around the room. Still nothing jumped out at her, though several of the spines of books on the bottom shelf were impossible to read without the office lights. *Maybe I can turn them on just for a moment.*

Then the clang again. She froze for several moments, waiting to see if the sound would come again. Suddenly, a long shadow fell into the office. Someone was just outside, walking past. If they didn't notice her, surely they would notice the book cart outside. The door never opened, and the shadow moved away. That was enough time sneaking about, she decided. This was too risky today. Maybe she could slip her keys to Trey, and he could come back tomorrow when Herman was alone and too busy to keep an eye on him.

As she stood to leave, she saw Evelyn's red notebook on the table. It only took a moment for her to decide to open it. She flipped through, seeing various notes in a shorthand that she didn't understand. But then she found the calendar in the back. It mostly contained what she would expect, but then she saw a pattern that made her blood turn to ice. The night before each body was found, there was a note for a private city council meeting. And on the day that each body was found, was the name of the victim.

The most recent meeting had been last night.

23

Trey awoke to the sound of knocking with the worst headache he had ever experienced. Everything from the neck up was on fire. He rolled to his side because he felt the urge to vomit wash over him. His whole body was wracked with chills. This might have been the worst he had ever felt.

The knocking continued, suddenly more insistent.

"Hold on," he croaked. His voice sounded like it was coming from torn vocal cords.

The knocking stopped, and the door swung open just as Trey puked into the little garbage can beside him. When he was done, he saw that it was Kevin sitting on the edge of his bed.

"What happened to you?" Kevin asked, covering his nose from the smell.

Trey sat up, realizing that he had gone to bed in his clothes.

"I don't know, I can't remember much from last night. Shouldn't you be in school?"

"It's Saturday," Kevin said with a smile. "That means it's officially a day past the first day you remember."

He chuckled at that, but Trey struggled to find the humor in it. Something about the date set his mind on fire, but everything was still so hazy. He knew that he had talked to Becca about her sister, but after that, he couldn't be sure.

"So what is it? What's got you busting in here all of a sudden?"

"I figured it out. Well, you did, or you covered it on your show, and that's how I figured it out."

Trey swung his legs off the side of the bed and held his head in his hands. He thought for a moment he was going to puke again, but he held it down.

"I'm struggling to follow, Kev," he said through clenched teeth. "Start at the beginning, please."

"Remember how I said I was pretty sure that the killer was being possessed by the Rootmother?"

Khythk'uhn.

The name rang out in Trey's mind, but he

didn't remember how he knew it. He nodded for the boy to continue.

"Well, I still think that's the case, but I think we were looking at it wrong. See, at first we—or I guess I should say I—thought that this killer was doing this because the victims were being sacrificed to the Rootmother. Then I listened to your episode where you mentioned Kenneth Knox, you remember what he wrote on the walls in his victim's blood?"

Trey did not remember. He shook his head.

"'We eat our young, just as they ate theirs,'" Kevin intoned. "So if I'm right, then that means that both men were possessed by something, the Rootmother here and probably something like her in the Knox case. They are carrying out a symbolic recreation of something that has happened before with these things.

"At some point in the past, they consumed their offspring. And I think that doing this turns the killer into a child of the entity. Get it? They will become the young, and then they will be the sacrifice themselves!"

Clearly, he had been connecting dots that Trey would have had a hard time following even if he felt normal. Nothing Kevin said made any sense, even by Jackson Point standards. Even if he was right about Knox and whoever was doing this here, how could they have any idea that the killer was meant to be the real sacrifice? And even worse, it didn't help them if he was right.

"Okay…" Trey said slowly. "And this does what, exactly? Does this help us find them? Does this help us stop them? I mean, shit, if you're right, then what? Does that mean they're gonna stop on their own and get gobbled up by some tree? Then this can happen all over again in a few years?"

Kevin looked crestfallen. It was clear that he had been very proud of his theory, as half-baked as it was.

"And even worse, Kev," Trey sighed, "we still have no idea who is doing this. That's what we need to figure out. What *I* need to figure out. You're just a kid. A very bright one, but just a kid, nonetheless…"

Trey trailed off. Flashes of the previous evening began to flood his mind. The drive, the sign, the date…*the tree*. Tears began to well up in the corner of his eyes. He remembered the despair. He remembered the fleeting moment of pain. He remembered the nothingness that came after.

"Trey?" Kevin asked, putting a hand on the man's shoulder. "Are you okay?"

"This is your fault," Trey whispered, his voice shaking with rage. "You lured me here when you knew what would happen. You knew I would be trapped here, along with everyone else, and you still asked me to come. How could you?"

"I'm sorry, Trey. I needed help, and nobody around here was going to do it. I thought that maybe together we could figure this out and—"

"And what, Kevin?!" Trey was shouting now. "What did you think we were going to do? Even if we stop this killer, then what? Huh? I'd still be stuck here. This isn't a goddamn fairytale! When we stop the bad guy, it doesn't break some magic spell. I'll still be stuck here!"

"Trey—"

"You shut the fuck up!" Trey screamed at the top of his lungs. "I died last night! I fucking died! My head was torn from my body, and I remember it! Do you have any idea what you've done to me?"

Kevin raised his hands to calm Trey, but it was too late. Trey straddled the teenager and began punching him in the face. First, his lip split, then one of his eyes swelled and closed. Finally, his nose shattered, covering both of them and the bed in blood.

"You trapped me in this podunk, backwater hell!" Trey screamed. "Does this hurt, Kevin? Does it? It doesn't matter! I bet tomorrow it won't even have happened. But I promise you this, it doesn't hurt as bad as having your head ripped off!"

"Enough!" Mrs. Best wheezed. "Get off my grandson and get the hell out of my house!"

Trey looked up to see the old woman holding an antique shotgun that was pointed right at him. He took a gulping breath and looked down at the shattered, bloody face of Kevin. For a moment, he was reminded of Chance and felt sick. He climbed off the boy and grabbed his things as quickly as he could, including his phone, which had somehow ended up back on the desk. Trey shuffled past the old woman who pressed the barrel of the gun into the small of his back.

"Trey," Kevin choked out. "I'm sorry! Please don't give up! Please."

"I already have!" Trey called back. "And so should you."

He slammed the door defiantly and dropped the key on the threshold. His car was sitting out front again, its front end caved in from the road sign, but otherwise undamaged. He got in, just started driving, not caring where he ended up or where the Rootmother would spit him back out.

Trey drove in circles around Jackson Point for hours. Every so often, he would glance at the library, but so far, he didn't have the courage to go in. He felt an odd mix of shame and anger still and wasn't sure that he could face Becca like this.

I should have listened, he thought. *She was right. I'm stuck here.*

Finally, he pulled into the drive-through at Tina's Tacos, just behind the fire department. Then he rolled over to the General Store and wolfed down the tacos in the parking lot, not caring that the grease dripped all down the front of him.

When the food finally settled and the adrenaline wore off, his mind started to clear, and he realized that he needed to figure out what to do next. He had nowhere to stay, and that needed to be his first priority; otherwise, he'd be forced to sleep in his car, and that would mean that he could easily become the next victim. No matter how he had felt the night before, he had no desire to die again.

Khythk'uhn.

There was that alien name again, the name that *Paganism & Pioneers* hadn't cared too much about. Somehow, Trey knew now that this was the true name of the Rootmother. She had a name not meant to be spoken by humans because she was older than them by a magnitude he couldn't fathom. Then his mind thought about something else mentioned about the Green Goddess that he had read: her crown was thought to be the stones that stuck out of the ground. So far, he hadn't seen them, but now he felt compelled to. But where were they?

He reasoned that they wouldn't be down one of the outlying roads or by the lake, or else the book would have said that. No—they had to be in the town itself, somewhere. But where hadn't he gone? Hell, today alone, he thought that he had driven up and down every block in Jackson Point.

All except one, he thought.

He had avoided most of First Street. He didn't want to go back to Chance's tree. To his tree. Something scratched at the back of his consciousness, telling him that he needed to go there. That had to be where the stones were. Trey threw his garbage out the window in one final act of defiance at the town and then headed back in the direction he didn't want to go.

A few minutes later, he was there, passing by the tree that had held two bodies in a single day. He forced himself to stare straight ahead, refusing to even look at the mighty pine. Though he was successful, his hands hurt from gripping the wheel so hard, and he felt sweat running down his back between his shoulder blades. The road only continued a short distance past the tree, where it stopped in front of a massive iron gate. On either side stood two tall brick walls that he couldn't see over.

Through the gate, he saw a mansion, larger even than Doc Thistle's house, which looked like it had partially burned down at one point. Vines, shrubs, and even trees had begun to take the mansion back into the forest generations ago, it seemed, and yet it still stood. He knew without needing confirmation that this had been the home of Frederick Ansel and the place where he had been killed.

Trey shivered, even as he opened the door of his car and got out to examine the gate. It didn't look like it was locked. He could enter if he so chose, a thought that gave him pause. Why was he so drawn to this place? It was like something was pulling him inside. He placed his hands on the gate and pushed them in. They swung open with a heavy creak, but that was all.

The grounds were full of leaves and pine needles. It looked like no one had even tried to walk through this place in decades—possibly since the man's body was recovered. In the center of the grounds, just in front of the house, stood a fountain. Water no longer ran through it, but thick black morass clogged the lower levels and gave off a foul odor. Trey continued on, as if in a trance.

The house itself was sprawling, a hodgepodge

of various periods and styles. It seemed to be a different size depending on the angle from which he looked at it. Most of the windows were cracked and shattered, but a few higher up were still intact. The color had once been a deep red, though now in many places it had changed to a mottled brown. All across it was marred with blackened stripes from the fire.

The front porch was sagging between the columns, but it held his weight. He stepped up to the thick double doors, themselves seemingly unmarred by either time or fire. Ornate wood-work in the shape of scrolls covered the doors. At the top of each was a stained-glass window. On the left side was a smiling face that looked to be made of wood, almost like that of a sprite. On the right side was the same face, but it looked angry and far more sinister. Trey's hand hovered over the doorknob for a few brief moments.

The stones, he thought.

For now, the spell was broken. He suddenly felt a chill again, and the smell of wet wood and other even more unsavory kinds of rot assaulted his nostrils. He ran back to his car, leaving the gate open. As he swung the SUV around, he saw out of the corner of his eye something large and gray through the trees behind the walls that sur-rounded the house.

That had to be it: *The Elder One's Crown.*

Seeing no alternative, Trey once again left the safety of his car and picked his way through the trees toward the stones. The trees grew tighter together as he walked, marking the end of the town and the beginning of the forest proper. Even though the stones had looked close to the road, the walk took Trey a good twenty minutes. Finally, out of breath and cut from various branches, he pushed his way into the clearing.

The stones themselves looked like giant chunks of basalt, reaching for the treetops like a cluster of fingers. They stood in a wide circle that could have easily fit a dozen cars inside. Trey pulled out his phone and started taking pictures of each stone. At first, they just looked like an odd rock formation, but as he got closer, he realized that something was very off about them. When he turned his head, it was like the angles of them changed. No longer did one part protrude, but now it seemed to recede, often at the same time. It was almost as if the entire Crown was an optical illusion.

Thinking he must be seeing things, he flipped through the photos on his phone. Not a single one caught the stones in focus. It looked as if each stone was affected by severe motion blur, even though everything else about the image was static and crisp. He tried one more time, and the picture came out the same.

Then a hand touched his shoulder. Trey screamed as he turned around. It was Mayor Tench who stood behind him with a reassuring smile. Out here in the woods, the man seemed even larger, and that made Trey very fearful.

"Mr. Savage," the mayor said. "What a surprise. When I saw your car on the road, I was afraid you had been foolish enough to go into Ansel's Mansion. Thank God you're out here, though I can't say this is much safer for an outsider."

"I came to see the Elder One's Crown myself," Trey said with confidence that he didn't feel. "I'd read about it and just wanted to see what all of the fuss was about."

"Is that so? Or were you trying to find another way out of town after you assaulted one of my citizens? A minor to boot!"

Trey felt his cheeks go red, but he said nothing. The mayor took a step closer, causing Trey to take a step back.

"I should have you locked up for what you did to the Anderhoff boy," the mayor said. "But I won't. Not yet anyway. For some reason, I think that you'd just cause even more trouble if I do that."

Trey decided to take the bait.

"Trouble like exposing your bullshit?" he asked, balling up a fist. "It's you, isn't it? You're the killer? Sacrificing these people to appease your Green Goddess, and using your cousin to help cover it up."

The mayor laughed, a deep belly laugh that seemed to echo off of the stones.

"You've been reading too many books, I think," he said. "I have never hurt a soul, Mr. Savage, though I might make an exception in your case."

Trey tried not to let the threat rattle him. Maybe it was having died and come back, or maybe it was the shame of what he had done to Kevin, but he had found his backbone again, and he didn't plan to lose it.

"If not you, then who? Hm? I know that people die all the time in this place. Sometimes they come back, sometimes they don't. I know that time is broken here because of the Root-mother, which I'm pretty sure is why no one can leave. So tell me, Tench...who is the killer if not you? Who was as much to gain keeping this place the way it is than the richest, most powerful little tyrant in town?"

The mayor turned his back on Trey and looked to be examining one of the stones up close. When he started speaking again, he didn't turn around.

"You know, people said the same thing about Ansel in his time. Some of my ancestors were probably spreading those rumors, too, I'll admit. They said he was the one causing the killings then, to make the camp and eventually the town prosper. It was bullshit then, and it's bullshit now. It may not seem that way to an outsider, but I love this community, even with its…flaws."

His face was calm when he turned back around, but his eyes simmered with controlled rage.

"Someone in this town is doing this, but it isn't me," the mayor said. "You might be right, and they might think this is what *she* wants, but I don't think so. I think she is satisfied with us nourishing her roots when our time comes naturally."

"She?" Trey asked. "Why won't you say her true name, Mayor? Especially here in her crown? Khythk'uhn?"

The mayor recoiled as if he had been cut when he heard Trey say that name.

"Where did you—"

"You think I'm the only one stuck here, but you forget, so are the rest of you."

Trey walked past the mayor and made the climb back to his car. By the time he got in, his heart was pounding. He took a breath to steady himself as he left the mansion and the woods behind. He knew where he had to go. The only place he would actually be safe.

24

Kevin sat at home the rest of the day with a bag of cold peas on his face. His mother wanted to call the sheriff and have Trey arrested, and his father hoped that he could find and kill the bastard himself, he said. Kevin told them both that he didn't want anything else to happen to Trey and that being trapped here was bad enough. Just like any other references to the broken time in Jackson Point, that shut them up.

After that, his mother went back to work at the real estate office, and his father back to the mill. Even though it was Saturday, it seemed Tench was pushing them extra hard. More and more trucks had been coming into town lately to pick up the lumber and take it around the state. His father said that once profits were up, they would all get raises. Kevin somehow doubted that.

As the day wore on, he tried to reason through his theory again. He knew he was right, he just had to figure out how to explain it to Trey. If they could find out who the killer was and complete the sacrifice, it was possible that no one else had to die. The Rootmother wouldn't find another host and start the process over again—not for a generation at least, as she would be satisfied. He couldn't explain it, but he knew it in his bones. His being a listener of *The Dead and the Undead* wasn't a coincidence. The answer was in the show. Trey had already figured it out without realizing it.

He took the peas off his face and went to the mirror. His entire face was varying shades of purple, his left eye was swollen completely shut, and his nose was broken. He should have gone to Doc Thistle's, but that place gave him the creeps. He told his parents it was because of what happened to Will Bainbridge, and they again let the matter drop. Kevin thought about what his classmates would say on Monday and sighed. The teasing would last the rest of the year, for sure. Then he thought about how much Ms. Moore would dote on him, and he perked up.

Ding-dong!

His doorbell went off, causing him to nearly

fall over in the bathroom. He tried to fix his messy hair and then realized it was the least of his worries and ran to the door. When he opened it, no one was there, but there was a folded piece of paper on his doorstep. Kevin looked up and down his block but didn't see anyone who could have left it, so he grabbed the paper and bolted back inside. When he opened it, he nearly dropped it in shock. It said:

Kevin,

I'm sorry about this morning. It's not safe for me to be out and about right now. Meet me at Christ's Cross at midnight.

-T.

Tears started flowing from Kevin's good eye. It wasn't over. They would figure this out together. He had snuck out before, so he wasn't worried about that. He was more concerned about making it to Christ's Cross in the dark. The local kids called the intersection by the church where Redeemer Avenue became Redeemer Place after crossing 5th Street, *Christ's Cross.*

The Anderhoff family lived on the far side of

town, up by the Douglas Fir restaurant. There wasn't one straight shot down there except for Crenshaw, and he didn't want to be in the open for that long.

Dammit Trey, he thought. *You could have at least offered to pick me up.*

His singular moment of frustration couldn't ruin his jubilation at the thought of Trey not being mad at him anymore, though. He grabbed a new bag of peas and ran to his bedroom, shutting the door. He decided that if he went to sleep now, his parents were unlikely to bother him when they got home. That would make sneaking out all the easier. Setting his alarm for 11:15, Kevin drifted off, thinking of what he would do to whoever killed Chance.

11:30 rolled around, and Kevin's parents hadn't bothered him once. He was already awake before his alarm, dressing himself in dark-colored sweats and a hoodie so that he wouldn't be seen. Popping the screen off of his window, Kevin hopped down into the shrubs and made a break for the sidewalk.

Once he was out of view of his house, he jogged down the street before cutting back into a neighbor's yard. He didn't want to spend too much time out in the open, but also didn't want to get shot trespassing on someone's property. This left him doing an awkward zigzag down Brickle, then over to Tench, where he did the same in the shadow of the mill. The giant structure cut a swath in the night sky, obstructing the stars like some kind of black hole.

He secretly hoped that he would never end up working there.

At the end of Tench Street, he followed 4th only halfway before beelining through the field that separated 4th from Redeemer Avenue. Up ahead, he could see the streetlights that marked Christ's Cross. To his right, Forest's Hope Church stood, its windows always alight, even in the middle of the night. He had never felt welcomed there, even though his grandmother was a member of the vestry. It wasn't necessarily Shepherd Cabot, but something else he couldn't put his finger on. Besides, they didn't like the way he dressed.

Finally, he was standing in the middle of the intersection, alone. He checked his watch, and it was 12:00 exactly. Maybe Trey had gotten lost?

How would that happen? He thought. *He chose the spot.*

Kevin heard a door open and close in the distance, and his heart stopped. In all of his excitement to meet Trey, he never once stopped to wonder how the outsider knew the name Christ's Cross. Realization washed over him like a wave, and he broke into an all-out run. Then he saw someone charging toward him from up the block. He turned and ran the opposite direction, toward Fincher Road, which led out of town to the rural families. That was the worst direction he could be running right now, but it was too late to change course again.

His breath came out in ragged bursts that made little clouds in front of his nose. Behind him, he could hear the heavy footfalls of a large man closing in on him. Kevin ducked to the left, making a break for the safety of the trees. He prayed that he could lose whoever this was and double back. Someone would let him in, and he could call Trey. It had to work.

Then he heard a crackling sound, like the breaking of a wet tree branch, followed by a low moan that turned into a growl. Kevin felt the urine run down his leg, but he had no time to register embarrassment. Whatever was chasing him, it no longer sounded human. Thick hands grabbed him by the shoulders and tossed him aside like he was weightless. The teenager slammed into a tree trunk, shattering his left arm.

"Fuck!" he cried out. "Help! Somebody help me! Trey! Mom!"

No one answered.

The dark shape towered over him, still growing with each snapping sound. It became taller and taller, as its shredded clothing fell away in tatters. In the last vestige of light, Kevin saw bright yellow on the ground, and in that moment, he knew who his killer was.

He was picked up again and impaled on a branch. By the time he saw it poking out of his stomach he had gone into shock.

"Trey..." he sighed.

Before he blacked out, he felt all-too-human teeth biting down on his toes.

25

The house burned all around it. Who had done this? Why was the cycle to be disrupted this way? It roared in anguish. The flames licked at its wooden flesh. The girl it held in its arms whimpered softly. It threw her into the wall with enough force to break her back. The wet thump her corpse made as it fell to the ground was nearly drowned out by the roaring of the flames.

Had the Elder One forsaken it? Was it now abandoned by Khythk'uhn? It tried to dig down through the floor for the safety of the earth, for the safety of her embrace, but it couldn't make it in time. A burning timber fell from the ceiling, smashing it into the ground. It let out one final cry of rage and was silent.

The dreamer hadn't truly slept. They had simply sat awake in bed until the hazy hours of the early morning had caused their mind to drift back to an older cycle, even if their body had never rested. This one had been the hardest so far. The Anderhoff boy didn't deserve this. But it had been her will, the others had said so.

The dreamer looked at the time and saw that church was only a few hours off. They needed to be ready to face the crowd. It was not yet time for their true nature to be revealed. That would come when the cycle was ended, and she was awake.

26

At the behest of Gideon—she hesitated to call him her boyfriend—Sam got ready for church that morning. It had been a long week, and Sunday seemed like it would never come. She hadn't been much of a church girl growing up, but she had taken to it here, if for no other reason than to hold onto something that felt normal. As normal as Forest's Hope Church could be, in any case. Its odd mix of fire and brimstone Christianity, along with whatever the hell the Rootmother beliefs were, had taken some getting used to. Now it was old hat, even if Cabot made her skin crawl.

She hadn't gone the last several Sundays, either too caught up in her research or too distracted by the killings. Still, she had made

Gideon a promise, and after the sex he had given her last night, she felt like she owed him. He was usually one of the first in the pews, sitting there by his lonesome sometimes, head bowed in prayer. As such, he had been gone before she had woken up to get there. Sam, on the other hand, would be lucky if she showed up before the singing started.

Sam put on a green dress with a matching hat that had a yellow flower on it. Looking in the mirror, she felt like she looked more like her mother every day. Once that would have pissed her off. Now it simply made her smile. When she was ready, she left her house and started her walk to the church. After all, why waste such a beautiful day?

About a block away from Forest's Hope, she heard the clang of the bells, announcing that the service was about to begin. Falling into line with the stream of other latecomers, Sam walked up the steps into a freshly painted white building. From the outside, it was a chapel in the traditional style, with a high steeple adorned with a simple cross. Inside, however, was quite different. The walls were vibrant with carvings of leaves painted green and golden boughs that reached into the recesses of the rafters. Stained glass windows of the forest lined every wall. The only depiction of Christ at all showed him nailed to a tree rather than a cross.

Once she was inside, she crossed to the front of the sanctuary and found her place in the front row beside Gideon. He smiled and gave her hand a squeeze before returning it to his prayer book. He was never one for impropriety, and a sexual affair between two unmarried teachers would have proven quite the scandal for the little town.

Once the bell stopped ringing, Shepherd Cabot rose and moved his way to the lectern to start the service. Sam looked around the room to take stock of the familiar faces she had missed in the last few weeks. She saw the Tench family on the other side of the pews, also in front. Behind them sat Clinton Abner and his wife, both of whom avoided eye contact with her. Eaton was there, sitting too close to one of his "girls". The Petersons behind them, Gloria Bainbridge by herself—poor thing—Evelyn McReedy, scowling at everything and nothing, and the Anderhoff and Best family, though there was no sign of Kevin. She felt a pang of concern but then ignored it. No mother would be sitting in church if her son were missing.

She was about to turn back to look at Shepherd Cabot when she noticed a pair of faces she had never seen on Sunday before: in the very back row, as if trying to avoid being noticed, sat Becca White, and the outsider, Trey whatever his name was. Sam thought that odd, seeing them here and together, but the pastor started speaking, so she turned back to the front.

"Blessed be the flock of the forest!" he began.

Sam wished she had brought her thermos.

When the service was over, the congregation filed out amidst the normal chatter one would expect in a small town. No one spoke of forest monsters or dead kids on Sunday. As she walked out into the sunlight—well away from Gideon so that no one suspected anything—Sam again noticed the Anderhoffs and Mrs. Best, so she walked over to check on Kevin.

"Mr. and Mrs. Anderhoff," she said cheerfully, "Is Kevin not feeling well this morning?"

Mrs. Anderhoff looked like she was about to say something, but her mother cut her off.

"He was beaten to a pulp by that outsider yesterday!" the old woman snapped. "I had to run him off with a gun!"

Sam rocked back on her heels. That wasn't what she was expecting to hear. Her head swiveled, looking for Becca White and Trey. If he had truly hurt Kevin, she planned to kick his ass here and now, Sunday or no Sunday. She saw the pair walking toward Christ's Cross and hustled after them.

"Ms. Moore!" Mrs. Anderhoff called after, but it was too late.

Sam caught up to the pair and turned Trey around in one smooth motion.

"Did you hurt one of my students yesterday?" she spat, venom dripping from every syllable. "Kevin?"

"Whoa, Samantha, calm down," Becca said.

"Shut the hell up, I wasn't talking to you," Sam responded. "Answer my damn question!"

"It's…complicated," the outsider said unconvincingly.

That was all she needed to hear.

"The fuck it is."

Sam punched Trey so hard that he toppled backward, sprawling on the road. Then she was on top of him, hitting him again and again. She felt Becca try to pull her off, so she jabbed her in the chest with an elbow and kept on hitting. It was finally Gideon of all people who pulled her off.

"Don't do this," he whispered in her ear. "Even with him as an outsider, do you really think *these* people will side with you over a white guy?"

She shook him off dismissively but shot him

a knowing glance that said, "Thank you." Under normal circumstances, she didn't need to have that kind of thing explained to her. But when her kids were involved, all bets were off.

Becca helped Trey to his feet. He was nursing his jaw like she might have broken it.

Good, she thought.

Then someone started screaming from the other side of the street. The crowd of church-goers ran in unison toward the sound. A woman had been walking her dog just beyond the tree-line, and she had come running out, carrying the little thing in her arms.

"It's awful!" the woman shouted. "Awful! They got another one! Another kid!"

Sam started running then, not caring who or what got in her way.

No, not another one. Not again, goddammit!

When she made it a few yards into the forest, she immediately saw him. High up on a branch that was protruding from his stomach was an-other teenage boy. His feet had been chewed off to his ankles, as had one hand and most of his face. It didn't matter. She knew who it was from the black nail polish on his fingers.

"No!" she screamed as she fell to her knees.

Moments later, the rest of the crowd fol-lowed, and Sam's wailing was joined by that of the boy's mother. Standing off to the side were Becca and Trey. The expression on the man's face was one of extreme shame.

He knew something, and she would find out what.

27

The headache had returned with a vengeance—either from his death or from the ass-kicking he had gotten that morning. Trey was lying down on Becca's couch while she changed in the other room. The pain was so all-encompassing that he couldn't even be bothered to visualize her naked a few feet from him.

After his run-in with the mayor the day before, Trey had come to Becca's trailer and waited on her porch until she got off work. For some reason, she didn't seem that surprised to see him there. He explained what had happened to him over the last twenty-four hours, and she agreed to let him stay. Trey slept on the couch while she took the bed, though both of them said good-night awkwardly enough that he figured he could have slept in her room if he had asked.

Sunday morning, one of them decided to go to church—Trey couldn't remember whose idea it had been. The thought was that Trey could get a better feel for the culture of the town, as well as possibly getting a moment alone with Kevin to apologize. Becca did warn him about the Best family, though, and the very real possibility that Kevin had only lured him to town to get another person trapped here and forced to buy a house from them.

Trey doubted her theory, doubly so after Kevin was found. The image of the dead teen was seared into his mind, far more so than even that of Chance. Kevin had simply been trying to avenge his friend and save his community. Even after trapping Trey here, he hadn't deserved that. *No one did.*

Throughout the day, Trey had regular panic attacks as he remembered the sensation of death. He hadn't slept much the night before, waking from dreams in which he was flying through the air toward that tree for what felt like hours. Even now, he struggles to regulate his breathing while his mind wandered. If he wasn't actively thinking through the case, he was remembering his death.

"Coffee? Ibuprofen?" Becca asked as she walked back into the room. She was dressed in black sweats and another loose-fitting shirt.

Trey sat up and nodded, setting the ice pack that he had been holding on his face aside. When she came back with a steaming cup and a handful of little red pills, he took both graciously, lying back with his eyes closed after swallowing the painkillers. Becca plopped onto the couch next to him and touched his swollen face tenderly.

"As purple as your face is, you still look pale," she said. "Which is it? Your death, or his?"

"Both," Trey whispered.

He didn't dare open his eyes for fear that she would take her hand away. Her skin was soft and smelled like peaches. That was something good he could focus on.

"Do you think there's a chance he could come back?" he asked.

"I don't know," she replied. "None of the ones who have died like this have come back—except when they were found again…and I don't think you want that."

"No…no, I don't. I just wish I hadn't ended it the way I did. He was just a kid."

"You can't hang onto that forever," she said, stroking his hair. "He knew what he was doing when he brought you here. Even if his intentions were good, he knew what he was doing."

"He just wanted me to find out who killed his friend."

"No, Trey. Chance died after you got here, remember? During your lost days. Kevin set this up with you days before that."

Trey felt a flash of rage for a moment, but it passed with another pang of pain. She was right. Sad as he was about the kid's death, Kevin had royally fucked him. Nothing could change that now. Not even death, it seemed.

"Now what do we do?" he asked himself just as much as her.

"The same thing we were doing. Find out who is doing this and stop them. Tomorrow we'll decide where to start and work on this together. At least we know that the city council—"

A loud bang on the door rattled the inside of the trailer. Then it came again and again, more insistent with each blow. Becca started to stand, but Trey motioned for her to wait. He wasn't about to let someone else get hurt. Taking a moment to compose himself, Trey threw open the door and raised a fist. What he was greeted with was the barrel of a silver revolver shoved directly into his face.

"Back up and be quiet," Samantha Moore said through gritted teeth.

Trey did as he was told, moving back to the couch beside Becca. Instinctively, he grabbed her hand, and they both stared at the other woman while she moved the recliner so that she could sit across from them. Without taking the gun off of Trey, she spoke.

"I want to know everything," she said coolly. "How you knew Kevin. Why you beat him up. What you know about his death. Start talking or I'll kill you both and walk right the fuck out of here."

Becca opened her mouth, but Sam swung the gun at her.

"I know you think you have the right to butt into everything," Sam said. "But you don't. I'm talking to Trey right now. If I need something from you, I'll let you know."

Becca squeezed Trey's hand harder and nodded. He could feel the small tremors in her arm.

"I knew Kevin because he was the reason I'm here. He listened to my podcast, *The Dead and the Undead*." Sam nodded in recognition and motioned with the gun for him to continue. "When the murders started, Kevin sent me a message and asked me to come out. He knew that I wanted to write a book about small-town serial killers, so it was an easy sell.

"I came to town on the 14th, which turned into the 15th and then the 18th and then the 16th and the 19th…you get the idea. I finally had enough and decided to leave, only I couldn't. When I…when I realized that I was trapped here, I killed myself. The next day, yesterday, I woke up fine, other than the horrific memory of my death. I was scared and angry, and I took that out on Kevin because he knew that by inviting me here, I would be stuck forever.

"As for what happened to him after that, I was as shocked as you—"

"No, no, you weren't," she interrupted. "I loved that boy. He was a good kid, possibly my favorite student. He was quiet, thoughtful, and a little strange. I wanted to keep my students safe most of all. Then you come to town, and two of them end up dead. Why? I know you have an idea."

Trey looked at Becca. She had stopped shaking and gave him a reassuring smile.

"You aren't from around here either, are you?" he asked.

Sam shook her head but didn't say anything.

"So I don't have to dance around you pretending that this Rootmother shit and time being all kinds of fucked up is normal. That's good. Well, so far I've found out a few things—or rather Becca and I have, Kevin too…

"First off, this has happened before. More than once, if I had to guess. For sure, it happened in the 1890s leading up to Frederick Ansel's death. I even think he was in on it, or at least knew enough to be the target of whatever is doing this. After Ansel's death, it seems that the killings stopped for a while. One thing I do know is that they were done to appease the Rootmother. Khythk'uhn."

Both women shivered at the name.

"Whatever this thing is, she is the reason time is broken here," Trey continued. "I think Ansel and some of the other town elders started a cult to worship her, a cult that is still happening today. Kevin was sure that the killer is being possessed by her, and that they are the true sacrifice, or will be once this batch of killings is done."

"And why did he think that?" Sam asked.

"It was mostly a hunch," Trey replied. "I didn't take him seriously until yesterday afternoon when I went to the Ansel mansion. Something there took over, and I nearly went inside without knowing why. After that, I went to the Elder One's Crown, and, well, look.."

He pulled out his phone and handed it to Sam. She set the gun across her lap and started swiping through the pictures. Something changed on her face then, but Trey couldn't figure out what it was.

"I don't know if you've been there, but something is off about those stones. The...angles aren't quite right. It's almost like they're in multiple places at once. And who did I run into there but Arthur Tench, your illustrious mayor. He threatened me, and I threatened him. Later that night, Kevin was killed. I don't think that's a co-incidence."

"You think Tench is behind this?" Sam asked, handing back the phone.

"I think it makes sense," Trey said. "His family took over the mill right after Ansel's death. To-day, they're the richest family in town, and the mayor and sheriff are Tenches to boot. It can't just be a coincidence."

"Can I speak now?" Becca asked, annoyance creeping into her voice once the gun wasn't pointed at them any longer. Sam nodded.

"I did some snooping myself, and I found a calendar in my boss's office showing that the city council had private meetings the nights before everybody was found. I think they're still partici-pating in the cult and ensuring that the mayor is being *taken over* or whatever is happening to make him do this."

Sam straightened and put the gun back in her waistband. She looked at them almost apologeti-cally before her face hardened again.

"I'd say I'm sorry for the gun, but I'm not. I had to be sure that I wasn't gonna be the next one stuck up in a tree. Now I know. Now it's time for me to share something with you.

"I'm not just a History Teacher. I went to col-lege for advanced mathematics, and I actually did research on the concept of fourth-dimensional beings. I'll skip the complicated parts—no offense—and get to what's important. I think this...*Khythk'uhn* is a fourth-dimensional being. She, or it, is so far beyond our understanding, it's nearly impossible to fathom. She exists on a higher plane, just like we do to a two-dimensional drawing.

"What we experience when we interact with her are basically just shadows that she is casting into the third dimension. That's why the stones seem impossible—because they are. They're shadows from her reality, not natural boulders from ours. That also explains why time is so fucked here."

Becca let out a low whistle. She was piecing it together faster than he was, it seemed.

"Okay, I think I'm following," Trey said. "But this is still some wild shit. Like...you actually believe this?"

"Any more wild than the fact that you know you died one day and were alive the next?"

"Point taken," Trey muttered. "Now what did you say about time?"

"A fourth-dimensional being would experience time much differently than us," Sam said. "We experience time in a linear fashion, but to her, it would be more like a single point. Past, present, and future—they all overlap at once in this place. That's why some days repeat and some don't happen at all. It's based around her perception, which means it's all fluid. Chance, Frederick Ansel, Kevin, even you, you are all alive and dead and dying all at once, right now, just as you always have and always will."

"Jesus Christ," Trey said.

"That's why…oh, Jenni," Becca whispered.

"I've been trying to keep track and study this since I got here, but the way all of the locals act like it's normal and mostly refuse to acknowledge it has made that nearly impossible."

"So, how do we kill a fourth-dimensional being?" Trey asked.

Sam laughed. Even though she was laughing at him, this put Trey at ease.

"We don't. That's like asking how someone kills God. You don't have any more of a chance of killing her than a kid's first stick figure has of killing you. What we can do, though, is stop her agents, break up her shadows, at least for a moment. That's what I hope, anyway."

"And what if time resets and it doesn't matter?" Trey asked.

"Then we do it again," Becca said. "And we keep doing it until it's done."

"Where do we start then?" Sam asked.

"With the city council," Trey said. "It's time they get to see the Rootmother's handiwork up close and personal."

28

Thankfully, the next day was Monday. Kevin wasn't found a second time, and Becca didn't have to go into the library. That gave them the time they needed to get their plan into action. Sam came over by 10, apparently having taken a leave of absence. She had brought all of her notes and her gun, Trey noted. Even though they were confident they knew who was doing this, Trey wanted to piece together as many of the facts as they could before they confronted them—little that would help with the sheriff likely being in on it as well.

The word was that Kevin was to be buried in the next few days at the small cemetery behind Forest's Hope Church. Mrs. Best had used her place in the vestry to ensure that a suitable plot was found. It was to be a small ceremony with only family present—which meant that the trio would have to mourn alone.

They started by spreading everything on the floor of Becca's trailer. First, they were looking for a pattern as to who the victims were. Had they been chosen at random, or was the council picking specific enemies to be dealt with?

The first body that showed up toward the end of September was Phillip Norris. Norris lived out toward Chinidere Mountain on a little homestead by himself. He wasn't that well known in town, and only ever came in once a week to buy supplies from Eaton's. The second had been found on October 1st. This time it had been a woman, a housekeeper for the mayor named Alicia Forsythe. Alicia's death was slightly different than the others. She had been found impaled, not on a tree, but on the statue of Frederick Ansel that stood in the public green behind City Hall. Next was Cillian Brickle on the 5th. Brickle was the descendant of one of the most prominent founders of the town, who had become the local drunk. Then came the youngest, a boy the age of three named Henry Fellows, on the 9th, and his older sister Marion on the 10th. Then there was a gap for almost a week until Chance and Kevin. Seven in all.

"I think we can guess that Alicia was killed because she knew something about the mayor,"

Trey said more confidently than he felt. "That explains why she was impaled in the green. She was a message more than a sacrifice. It's hard to say why the others had been chosen."

"Other than Kevin," Sam added.

"Other than Kevin," Trey agreed.

They didn't have photos of any of the corpses besides Chance, so Trey had to rely on the memories of the two women to form a picture of what had happened to them. The town had been hit the hardest by the deaths of the children, of course. Henry and Marion went missing at the same time, though they were found a day apart. Trey felt it was obvious that they had been taken and killed at the same time, though why they weren't left together, he had no idea.

He laid a map out on the ground in front of them and marked each of the places where a body had been found. The six corpses that had been impaled on trees had formed a loose circle around the borders of the town. The exact shape looked familiar to Trey, but he couldn't think of exactly why, yet. The placement of the other six definitely made Alicia's body stick out all the more. But why did the mayor need to send a message, and to whom?

Something isn't adding up, he thought.

"We need to go back to Ansel's mansion," he said finally.

"Are you nuts?" Becca asked. "That might be the least safe place in town."

To Trey's surprise, Sam was shaking her head too.

"I tried to go there once after I first got here. We won't find anything good there."

Trey remembered his own experience from two days ago—the feeling of some other presence taking over his mind and trying to draw him in. Still, he wasn't going to back down. Not after what had happened to Kevin.

"We have to," he said. "This has happened before, we know that much. And the best chance of finding any records of what finally ended it is in there. Unless you want to force your way into the council chambers at gunpoint?"

"You're nuts," Sam said with a smirk.

"When I was growing up, a few boys dared each other to go in there to prove how brave they were," Becca whispered. "Only one came back, and he had to be put into one of Thistle's padded rooms. They never even sent a search party for the others. They just pretended that they never existed."

Sam clenched her fists before taking a deep breath to steady herself.

"The legend is that he kept building the house up until his death," Becca continued. "Adding rooms that no one ever saw the inside of. The builders claimed that the layout of the house was impossible, and that entire wings of the house that they had built one year would be gone the next. It just isn't *right*."

"So it sounds like the whole house is one of your shadows, doesn't it, Sam?" Trey asked.

"I guess so. That would make sense since it's so close to the Crown," she whispered in reply.

"Whether Ansel was a victim or the killer in his time, we need to know what happened to stop this, and we need to do it today, before the next body is one of ours," Trey said. "They killed Kevin because we were getting too close. The way I see it, we don't have more than a few days left."

The women both nodded in sullen agreement.

"Good, so let's get going," Trey said. "And bring the gun."

The trio didn't make it off the porch before the squad car rolled up. Sheriff Tench and one of her deputies got out with guns already raised. Trey and the others raised their hands before any instructions had even been barked out.

We're too late, Trey thought. *Fucking Christ.*

"Treyton Savage," Tench shouted. "You are

under arrest for the murder of Kevin Anderhoff, and God help me, the other six victims if I can prove it."

"What are you talking about?" Becca asked indignantly. "Trey was with me the night Kevin died, and he wasn't even in town for five of the others."

"We found a note in Kevin's home asking him to meet Trey at Christ's Cross."

The deputy roughly grabbed Trey and dragged him to the squad car, where they cuffed him. Moments later, he was being shoved into the back seat again. Before getting back into the driver's seat, Sheriff Tench looked at Sam for a long while.

"Sam," she said. "I hope you choose better company in the future."

Then she was in, and they were driving away. Trey watched as the trailer receded behind him, with both women staring after them in shock.

✺

"You know I couldn't have done this," Trey said.

He was still cuffed, though his hands were in front of him now. Sheriff Tench was sitting across from him at her desk, riffling through a manila folder. After a few moments, she slapped several photographs of Kevin's corpse on the desk in front of him. Trey tried to look away; he had already seen it in person and didn't need to see it again.

"Beating him wasn't enough, was it, Savage?" she asked. "You had to live up to your name and eat the poor kid? He didn't lure you here, did he? You came on your own, to find a place to live out a sick fantasy just like the ones you covered in your little podcast."

Trey swallowed hard and looked around the station. There didn't seem to be an interrogation room, but there was a cell with a single cot at the far side of the room.

"I want a lawyer," he said defiantly.

Tench snickered..

"You really think we've got a lawyer in this town? What the fuck kind of lawyer would move here? Huh? We don't have any lawyers, we don't have any judges, and we don't do trials."

"So you just lynch people, eh?" Trey spat. "Surprise, surprise from a racist hicktown thug pretending to be a cop."

If his accusations rattled her, she didn't show it. Instead, she pulled something else from the folder, a scrap of paper that she set on top of the pictures. Trey stared at it with a mix of guilt and revulsion.

Kevin,

I'm sorry about this morning. It's not safe for me to be out and about right now. Meet me at Christ's Cross at midnight.

-T.

Trey would have laughed at the absurdity of the note if it hadn't gotten Kevin killed. He never would have signed something with the letter B, nor did he even know the name of that intersection until after Kevin died.

"That's not even my handwriting," he said. "Compare it to my notebooks."

Tench sighed and rubbed her temples.

"Look," she said quietly. "You are clearly one fucked-up son-of-a-bitch, but if you confess I'll make sure you go out quick. One to the back of the head in the woods, and it's over. Hell, if you come back, I'll find some other way to do it that's less...violent. Get the Doc to put you to sleep or something.

"But if you keep up this charade, and I have to present evidence against you at the town hall, you aren't gonna like what they do to you."

"You said you don't do trials here," Trey whispered.

"It's not a trial, so much as a public execution."

"How do I know that note was even found in Kevin's house? The way I see it, you probably wrote it yourself to cover for your cousin, who you know is the real killer."

Tench backhanded him then, splitting his lip and causing the bruising on his face to throb again.

"My cousin is many things, but he ain't a killer," she hissed. "My family has watched over this town since it was three tents and a campfire."

"You mean you've followed the will of the Rootmother?" Trey whispered. "Khythk'uhn."

Just as her cousin had, the sheriff recoiled at the true name of the Green Goddess. Then she stormed off, shouting to her deputies to go back to Becca's and grab his notebooks.

Another hour crept by before she returned, dumping his backpack over the top of the photographs. The sheriff knocked most of the things to the floor before she settled on the Moleskine. Forged note in hand, she flipped through page by page, closely comparing the handwriting. Several agonizing minutes later, she dropped the notebook in exasperation.

"Get me keys," she shouted to a deputy.

"What?" the man asked. "Are you sure, Sheriff?"

She didn't answer, but she did nod. Her eyes met Trey's, and it almost looked as if she had tears in them.

"I don't know what is happening to my town," she whispered. "But I won't have another innocent die because of me. Get the fuck out."

Trey gathered his things and ran all the way back to the trailer park. They still had to get to the mansion before it was too late.

29

The gates of the Ansel Mansion still hung open, just as Trey had left them. The trio stood next to the fountain in the growing shadows of the perimeter wall. All three felt the overwhelming pull of the place to step inside. Becca and Sam looked even more uncomfortable than Trey felt. That gave him the push he needed to say what he had been thinking since he got out of the police station.

"I'm going in alone," he said. "You two go check out the crown and see if you notice anything I didn't."

"No way," the women said in unison.

"If it's as dangerous as we think, we can't risk all three of us," Trey whispered. "Besides, I've already died once. Doing it again wouldn't be the worst thing."

He felt the rush of air before his head was ripped from his shoulders. He still hadn't told them the worst part: that he had been aware for several minutes before his brain had finally shut off. Several minutes that he stared at his own headless body with unblinking eyes. Real death sounded like a release to him now.

"Hand me the gun," he said, holding out his hand.

Sam handed it over, giving him a look that seemed to ask if he knew how to use it. He didn't, but he wasn't about to tell her that. With one final nod to the others, he tightened the straps on his backpack and walked up the steps, putting his hand on the doorknob.

Inside, the mansion was ice cold. Bits of scattered sunlight tore through holes in the walls and ceiling, revealing dust motes from a hundred years of abandonment. Even after all this time, the place still smelled like smoke.

Trey took two uneven steps forward on the creaking wood. The force that had tried so hard to pull him in now seemed to wish to keep him out. It was as if he was suddenly made of lead, and he feared he would fall through the floor at any moment.

The entryway opened into a grand hall, with three separate stairs, each leading to a different floor. Doors lined each wall, some open and some closed—none inviting. He gripped the gun tightly in his right hand, the sweat already making it slick in his palm. They were right, this place was wrong. Turning back as he was overcome with fear, Trey pulled the front door back open.

Outside, the grounds no longer looked abandoned. The leaves and pine needles were all missing, and the fountain gently bubbled fresh, clean water. In the distance, he could hear the steady thumping of an axe against a tree. Taken aback, Trey pushed himself back into the mansion and slammed the door. He was back in the rotten shell of the building, and as far as he could tell, the present.

This was a mistake, he thought sourly. *Great job, dumbass.*

He reasoned that what he was looking for had to be in one of the rooms above. A man like Ansel likely roomed on one of the upper floors. Trey was hoping that the town's progenitor had left behind a journal or something that would give him a hint as to how to stop this.

Trey settled on the widest staircase directly in front of him. It was made of a cherry-colored wood that still seemed to shine beneath the layers of dust. Up the center of the stairs ran a decaying purple carpet. He gripped the railing on the left side and forced his legs to work, moving up one slow step at a time. The inside of the mansion was deathly silent, other than the creaking of the stairs. Trey tried to keep his breathing quiet. He didn't know how, but he could tell that he wasn't alone in here.

At the top of the stairs, the landing wrapped around both to the left and the right, terminating on each side with a wide hallway. Unlike in the Doctor's house, no signs pointed the way to his destination. He sighed and chose the left hall as it was closest.

This side of the house seemed to have been spared from the worst of the fire. That also meant that there were no holes to let in any light. Trey pulled out his phone and turned on the flashlight. Candlesticks and paintings hung from the walls between the doors, along with a density of cobwebs that made his skin crawl. Still, he continued on, refusing to try any door until he was sure that he had found the correct room. When he reached the end of the hall, a large gridded window divided with rusted black mullions shed some faint light into the hall. Trey looked out at an overgrown garden below. It seemed that the outside was the present once more—that was something, at least.

None of the doors here seemed to be for a master bedroom, so he made his way back to the other side and started the process over. This hall had seen the worst of the fire; nearly half of the hall itself was missing its ceiling, which allowed Trey to see, but also forced him to crawl over the uneven floor where the collapsed roof lay in dusty piles.

Near the end of this side, the chunks of wall were missing, as were the doors of the final two rooms. Something told him that this was what he had been looking for. The fire had started here, from what he could tell, and he knew that meant it had been intended to kill Ansel.

On the left, the room itself barely remained. Nearly half of the floor was missing, and what remained looked to be crumbling away. Every inch of wood that remained was scorched a dark and brittle black. In the center of the room was a melted pile of brass that Trey assumed had once been the bed of Frederick Ansel. He tried to creep forward, but the groaning of the floor gave him pause. Instead, he turned back to investigate the room across the hall.

It seemed to be in better shape, though it was also missing part of its external wall. This room had clearly been the man's study. What was left of the walls were the scattered remains of bookshelves, though their contents had long since been destroyed—either by the fire or the elements. In the center, however, sat a large oak desk that seemed to have been mostly untouched.

Trey tested the floor first and found it to be much more solid in this room. Even so, he crawled across it on his belly as if he were trying to cross a frozen lake. When he made it to the desk, he slowly pulled himself up and began looking through the drawers. Inside the top center drawer was a small leather book. Slowly, so as not to break the cover, Trey opened it. To his excitement, it looked to be a journal. He slipped the book into his backpack. He wanted out of this place as quickly as possible.

No sooner had he taken his first step back toward the door, the floor gave way with a thunderous groan, and he plunged into the darkness below.

30

Becca and Sam carefully made their way through the forest to the cluster of stones. Neither had ever been there. Becca had been too scared after the stories she had heard as a child, and Sam had been unwilling to go this far away from the center of town alone.

The trees finally gave way to the small clearing, just as Trey had described it. The large stones protruded from the earth in a way that made Becca feel uneasy. They didn't look like they had gotten there by random geologic activity, but more like something had forced them to the surface all at once. Something that they might still have been connected to.

"We should go," she whispered to Sam. "I think this was a bad idea. She might be under these, for all we know."

"She's probably everywhere," Sam said. It wasn't reassuring. "The fourth dimension doesn't line up neatly with the third."

"When you reduce it to math, it doesn't sound as scary," Becca said. "Stop that. We need to remember what we're actually dealing with here. You know, a *god*."

Sam nodded but didn't respond. She was too busy staring in awe at the impossible shapes made by the rocks. Trey had been right, the angles didn't seem possible. It was like they pointed outward and inward in the same places. Depending on how she looked at them, Becca thought they were so narrow they could have been flat, and then other times they seemed so wide that they were all she could see. It was disorienting, to say the least.

She sat down in the middle of the stones and tried to close her eyes to see if the dizziness would subside. It didn't. So she tried something else. Becca started counting the stones. There were seven. Then she tried looking at the ground, but it just seemed to spin under her, as if she was unanchored here, experiencing the rotation of the globe at an impossible speed.

"I need a moment," she said.

"Go for it," Sam replied, not really paying attention to her.

Becca walked out of the circle and sat on a

natural rock, looking out at the forest. Through the trees, she could make out the unnamed road that ran along this place. No one had ever wanted to give a name to the dirt road that headed up toward Tomlike Mountain. It ran too close to the Ansel Mansion and the Crown, so it wasn't worth using, and if it wasn't worth using, it wasn't worth naming.

The dizziness went away after a few minutes, thankfully. Being away from the Crown and breathing in the smell of pine had been enough. The wind was getting chilly again, and the sun had started to get lower in the sky. They needed to get going soon, which meant that Trey needed to hurry up and get out of that damned placed.

She reached into her bag and pulled out the map of the town that they had marked the bodies on. If she couldn't look at the stones, maybe she could figure out some other part of the mystery. Becca marked each "x" with a finger, working her way in a circle around Jackson Point. Seven bodies but only six on trees. She figured that meant only six had been actual sacrifices. But there needed to be seven. *Seven.*

"Oh shit!" she exclaimed.

"What is it?" Sam called from inside the stones.

"Stay there!"

She tried to ignore the spinning as she stumbled back into the Crown. Sam walked over just as Becca placed the map on the ground. The x's match the positioning of each stone, all but one.

"There's gonna be one more," she said.

"We've gotta get Trey," Sam whispered.

31

The floating dust looked like thick clouds as it rolled about the room. Trey shook his head and sat up, looking around the dim place he had landed. His tailbone hurt, but he didn't think anything was broken. He stood and brushed the dust from his front. Thankfully, the gun was right next to him.

Well, he thought. *At least I don't have to take those stairs again.*

He fumbled with his phone for a moment before he got the light back on. Directly across from him was the only door that led out of this room. It was impossible to tell what it had been, long before he had fallen into it. Bits of floor and desk, and dust covered everything now. Trey sighed and pressed on, opening the rotting door slowly and peeking out into the hall.

It looked nearly like the hallway above had, but it hadn't faced the same damage from the fire. At the end of the hall, he could see the faint light of the central room. He was close to getting out of here and finding Becca and Sam. When they got back to the trailer, they would read Ansel's journal and figure out what to do next. He had to believe that. *He had to.*

Just before the end of the hallway, something flashed in the corner of his eye. He turned and saw light leaking from under the closest door; not the light of the sun, but the light of modern bulbs. Every ounce of him wanted to run. He knew that nothing good could be behind that door. There was no way that any part of this house had working, modern electricity, and yet he could see it.

Ignoring his fear, Trey grabbed the doorknob and slipped through the opening into the brightness beyond.

On the other side of the mansion door, Mayor Tench sat behind an antique desk with a glass top. An older computer sat atop the desk, as well as one of those annoying bird figures that moved up and down to mimic the bird drinking. Trey walked into the office, dumbstruck. The mayor didn't see him at first until the door clicked shut behind him.

"What the hell?" the large man asked. "How did you get in here?" Then the mayor noticed that the dust and ash that covered Trey head to toe, and added. "And where have you been?"

"I went back to the mansion," Trey said quietly. "*She* must have brought me here."

"What are you talking about?"

"The Rootmother brought me here. It has to be."

Then Tench noticed the gun gripped tightly in Trey's shaking hand.

"Now let's calm down, Savage," he said.

Trey mechanically raised the gun toward the mayor, pulling the hammer back like he had seen in the movies.

"I spent all this time figuring out how to stop you, and she just sent me here to do it the old-fashioned way. That must mean that your sacrifices aren't what she wants. Have you ever died before, Mayor? Let me tell you, it's as horrific as you would imagine, but waking up the next day is even worse."

Tench raised his hands over his head. For the first time, Trey saw that the man's forehead was glistening with sweat.

"I told you before," the mayor began, "that I didn't do this. My family has always protected this town. Yes, we revere the Rootmother. How could someone who spent their whole life here not? But we don't make sacrifices to her."

"Bullshit!" Trey shouted, waving the gun for emphasis. "We know that the council has had private meetings every night just before a body has been found. That's when you all decide who to kill, isn't it? You killed your maid because she overheard something, and Kevin, because we were getting too close. The others were just chance, weren't they?"

A look of recognition seemed to pass over the mayor's face, but then it was gone.

"You're wrong, Trey," he said slowly. "You're close, but it's not me. I've been trying to stop it."

"Then who is doing this? You still haven't even had the balls to throw someone else under the bus!"

Tench shifted uncomfortably in his seat but kept his mouth shut.

"That's what I thought."

"Wait!" Tench shouted. "Think about it! Think! My family has always viewed this town as our responsibility. The people here are like our children. Why would we eat our young?"

"Jesus Christ," Trey said. "Kevin was right."

He squeezed the trigger. The thunderclap of the pistol rang out in his ears. The mayor snapped backward, his chest blooming a scarlet circle.

"If you come back tomorrow, I'll just do it again," Trey whispered before walking out the door.

Trey walked back into the mansion, the gun heavy in his hands and his ears still ringing. It was over. The killer was gone. The three of them would still need to do something about the city council—Trey wasn't convinced that they couldn't simply make another vessel, but at least for a day or two, this would stop.

No longer caring about the noise he made, he ran back through the main hall and stumbled out onto the front porch. He was still in the present. Becca and Sam were standing by the fountain, close to where he had left them.

"We have to go," he said. "I found a journal, and…" he trailed off, not sure what they would think about him killing the mayor in cold blood.

"There needs to be seven sacrifices!" Becca exclaimed. "The bodies, they line up with the stones in the Crown. The maid wasn't one, you were right. We have to stop them before they do the seventh."

"What happened in there?" Sam asked, her eyes suddenly sharp.

"I fell," Trey said, handing her the gun with distaste. She popped the cylinder to check the rounds.

"And what did you shoot?" Sam asked.

"Huh?"

"One of these shells is spent, so I ask again, who did you shoot?"

Trey kept walking toward the car.

"The mayor. Come on, we've still got work to do."

The women followed him in a stunned silence. There was no turning back now.

32

Instead of the trailer, they went back to Sam's house for fear that Becca's wasn't safe any longer. Not that it would take the sheriff long to come here, given that she had seen them together. Once they got settled in, the three of them sat in stunned silence for several minutes. Sam eventually got up and made the group a frozen pizza while Trey stared at the gun where it was sitting on a side table, and Becca pored over the map, trying to guess where exactly the last body would end up.

Trey's head was aching again. He kept seeing himself crashing into that tree, but when he tried to ignore the mental image, it was replaced with the mayor dying. Who had he become? He'd never even held a gun before, and now he was a murderer.

Finally, over crappy pizza and few beers, they got to work looking through Ansel's journal. It was mostly a collection of notes about consolidating power in the camp, and racist rants about "negros" and "chinamen". Eventually, though, the passages became more erratic, and the handwriting started to slip from its original clean lines to near scribbles while the passages grew shorter and shorter. Trey read aloud a few choice passages that he thought were relevant:

July 16th, 1888

What a strange place this has become. My days repeat, and my desire to leave grows dimmer with every passing hour. I cannot recall when I first came here. Some of the others have tried to flee after that business in the woods last month, but I never heard what became of them.

I don't care, the mill has made me enough money, I can always just buy more workers.

August 11th, 1890

I can hear her in my head at all times now. I am never alone. I never have been since finding this place, truth be told. But now, she whispers to me as I wake, and I dream of her when I sleep.

April 5th, 1894

The house is nearly done, and yet I know it's not what she wants. I will need to make it anew. The men won't care if I pay them enough.

October 21st, 1896

He came back today. Claiming still to be my son. The fool could ruin everything.

September 30th, 1897

He has turned them against me. They want to talk to her as I do. I have caught them at the stones, chanting in the night. I will find a way to stop them.

October 7th, 1897

Another body was found. This thing will be the death of us all. They have done this, and I must put a stop to it. The cycle cannot be completed.

October 14th, 1897

I now know what it is and how to stop it. Not all of her children can be killed with fire, but this one can. My bullets killed the man last night, but not the beast. I have brought a child here to lure it. One that they had chosen to be the seventh. The cycle ends with me.

"Holy shit," Becca said.

"Holy shit is right," Sam echoed.

They all sat quietly again, finishing the last slices of pizza that had gone cold while Trey had been reading. There had been quite a bit of other strange things in here, but he didn't have the time or the brain power to try and filter through them all. This had to be enough, for now.

"I'll just go ahead and say what you're thinking," he began. "If I was right about the mayor, shooting him wasn't enough, or else Ansel wouldn't have burned his house down. We have to trap him somewhere tomorrow and burn it down. Preferably with the council inside."

"Now hold on," Becca said, holding up her hands. "I agree with you that the council is behind this. I found out about their meetings, remember? But I think we need a better plan than burning a handful of people alive. We need to *know*, for sure. You shooting the mayor today was probably the dumbest thing you've done since you decided to drive to Jackson Point."

"Becca's right," Sam said. "We don't know as much as you think we do. We don't know what will happen if they really finish this 'cycle', for one thing. Maybe nothing. Maybe this was all a waste, and she doesn't wake up."

"So you think we wait for another person to die, and just see what happens?" Trey asked, annoyance creeping into his voice.

"No," Sam replied. "I'm saying we need to get one of these motherfuckers to talk before we blow someone else's head off. We don't know shit. We have an idea, but we don't actually know anything concrete, and that should make you take a step back."

"He said the same thing about eating their young that Kenneth Knox did!" Trey protested.

"What?" Becca and Sam asked together.

"Kevin was right. The people getting killed aren't the real sacrifice. The killer is. He has to kill the seven people and place them in the formation Becca figured out, and then they'll kill him at the Crown! It's just a reenactment of some ancient rite performed by Khythk'uhn!"

"Now you sound like the crazy one," Sam said. "You know that, right? I loved Kevin, but I'm not placing all of my faith in the detective skills of a seventeen-year-old."

"Me either," Becca whispered.

"Then what?" Trey asked. "We have to kill this piece of shit for real before the cycle ends, or else who knows what'll happen. We have to. So I say we go and find one of the council members now."

There was a faint knock on the door.

"Sam, it's Gideon," a voice called.

"Fuck," Sam whispered.

She stood and hid the gun under a pillow. She opened the door, and a large bald man stepped inside. He looked at Trey and Becca with a glare of disapproval.

"When I said you should be careful, I didn't mean to shack up with these two..." he said.

"It's not what you think," she protested. "We're trying to figure out who hurt Kevin and—"

"The mayor is missing," Gideon said sharply. "No one knows where he is. People are scared. Just—please stay inside tonight. And send these two somewhere else."

He stormed out with Sam chasing after him.

"Wait!" she shouted. "You told me that you had a theory about who was doing this! Who do you think it is, Gideon?"

"After tomorrow, it won't matter," he replied just before a car engine started.

Sam walked back in and slumped down on the couch, defeated.

"What did he mean by that?" Becca asked.

"He meant that just because you're fucking somebody, it doesn't mean you really know them," Sam replied.

None of them slept well that night. Trey had the same dream about Becca as he had before, but this time she ripped his head off after they finished having sex, while the mayor watched from the doorway. When he awoke, covered in sweat on the floor of Sam's front room, he didn't immediately try to go back to sleep and instead listened to old episodes of his show. Normally, he didn't like the sound of his own voice, but tonight it was comforting to hear himself before everything got so fucked up.

The next morning, they were all awakened by the ringing of Sam's doorbell. Trey and Becca sat up, bleary-eyed.

"Doesn't anyone use a phone in this god-damned town," Trey complained.

"Nobody with something important to say," Sam said as she raced to the door.

Trey grabbed the gun and hid it under his blanket. He checked his phone and saw that it was Monday again. Sam opened the door, and both the mayor and the sheriff forced their way inside before she could say anything.

"Savage," the mayor said. "It's time the five of us had a chat, and preferably without me getting shot this time."

33

They all sat around Sam's table, each with a cup of steaming coffee in front of them. Trey and Becca were still both in shirts and underwear, while Sam had at least changed into sweats. Trey felt horribly underdressed compared to the Tenches.

"I could arrest you for murder this time," the sheriff spat.

"Good luck, since it didn't stick," Trey shot back.

"Nance, please," the mayor said. "We didn't come here to stir up shit. It's past that. Listen, it's time we came clean to you about everything. I think working together is the only way we can stop this madness."

"I'm still not convinced it's not you, but we're

listening," Becca said, giving Trey's hand a reassuring squeeze.

"If it were me, you three wouldn't have lasted the night," the mayor said coolly.

"As it is, you're lucky I found him before anyone else," the sheriff interjected. "How his secretary didn't hear the shot, I'll never know. I snuck his body out in the middle of the night and hoped he would come back today. I couldn't let them know what happened."

Trey and the others stared at the Tenches impassively.

"Let me start at the beginning," the mayor said, sipping his coffee. "Long before we settled this land, hell, even before the Indians did, other things realized there was power in these woods. Power in other places, too. They started to worship those places and commune with the gods buried beneath the earth.

"Eventually, humans came along and took after the others. They formed cults to worship the gods. Many of which were nameless. People started gathering in these places. Not many, mind you. The power of these places kept most away, but some were drawn to them. That's what happened here. The first Tenches and that fool Ansel were drawn here. The difference was, the Tenches already knew what they would find in these woods.

"They were members of a cult called The Fifth Signet. They had been finding and worshipping Old Ones the world over, in Nexus Towns just like Jackson Point. Some of whom are far more powerful than even Khythk'uhn."

Trey tensed, as did Becca. Sam's eyes moved toward the blanket where Trey had left the gun.

"Don't worry," the sheriff cooed mockingly. "Our family broke off from The Fifth Signet a generation back. They hate us now, about as much as they hate you."

"We've had a...tenuous peace," the mayor continued. "Until now, that is. These sacrifices come in cycles, as I'm sure you've learned. And you were right about who is in the cult now. Evelyn McReedy, Clinton Abner, Shepherd Cabot, the rest of the city council, and a few others. I confronted them after Phillip Norris was killed. They retaliated by killing Alicia. I've been trying to find a way to destroy their creature and bring them down, but so far it has alluded me. None of my family records have any indication of how to stop this...for obvious reasons."

"Fire," Trey croaked. "You can kill it with fire. Ansel figured that out. I got his journal from his mansion right before I..."

"Ah," the mayor said. "Well, that is a blessing then. I take it that the Rootmother *did* bring you here for a reason."

"How can you still worship her, after she's caused all this?" Becca asked.

"Doesn't the Bible say the Lord works in mysterious ways?" the mayor asked. "We don't disagree with The Fifth Signet about the power of Khythk'uhn, only in the manner of worship. I don't want more of my people to die. That brings me to tonight."

"Tonight?" Sam asked, still eyeing the blanket.

"Tonight will be the final feeding, and then they can give the Rootmother back her son. If we can destroy him before that happens, this stops."

"And if we don't?" Trey asked.

"We don't know for sure," the sheriff said. "These 'cycles' as they call them, have been going on since before humanity. At some point, they're supposed to awaken the Green Goddess, and she shall bring about the end of the world. That could be this time, or another. We can't be certain."

"Again, why would you want to stop this?" Becca asked, more insistent this time.

"When the stars are right, they're right," the mayor said quietly. "We don't think it's up to humans to force the issue. Especially not at the expense of children."

"We know the where and the when," the sheriff explained. "Tonight at the Crown, they aim to finish this. We have...a man on the inside."

"Oh really?" Trey tried not to roll his eyes.

"Clinton Abner," the mayor said.

Sam gripped her mug so hard that Trey was sure that she was going to break the handle off.

"He's a snake and a coward," the sheriff said. "I cornered him last night and stuck my gun so far down his throat I could've blown a hole in his stomach. He told me everything except who the son actually is."

"So who's the victim gonna be, then?" Trey asked.

"Well, I am," the mayor said. "And I want you four to stop them before I get killed."

34

Becca walked alone through the aisles at Eaton's; what the locals called the General Store since the owner was Eaton Marsh. Trey and Sam were too conspicuous right now, so they had stayed behind at Sam's house. Arthur and Nancy Tench went back to their normal business so as not to draw attention to themselves. The mayor expected he would be taken just after sundown from his house and dragged off to the Crown, the location of the last X on Becca's map. Even though Abner had revealed the plan, he wouldn't dare warn the others, or they'd kill him too.

That meant that the remaining four needed to be ready to stop the ritual by sundown. That meant they needed to be ready to burn that son of a bitch, whoever he was. Which brought

Becca here. She slowly rolled her cart around the store, trying to hide some of the more incriminating items amidst innocuous ones. She had cereal, four lighters, bread, jam, eggs, a gas container, some bleach, laundry detergent, a few rags, and a six-pack of beer in bottles.

Eaton was thankfully nowhere to be seen. The old man was on the city council and a pervert to boot. He only employed young girls fresh out of school, and he was known to touch them inappropriately from time to time. No one said anything because of his political position. Becca aimed to set him ablaze tonight as well if she got the chance.

"Hi Carrie," Becca said to the cashier, a regular at the library.

"Oh, hi Becca!" Carrie squealed. "You know, I couldn't put that book down, the one you recommended about the—"

Becca smiled and nodded along, but had completely tuned Carrie out. She was too worried that the girl would ask her about the contents of her cart. Thankfully, the questions never came. The two said their goodbyes, and Becca walked back out to her car. She got everything into the trunk and slammed it shut, just as Gideon Nelson, the school Gym Teacher and apparent fuck-buddy of Sam's, approached her.

He was wearing his usual blue tracksuit and garish shoes.

"Becca, right?" he asked, as if he didn't know.

"Mr. Nelson, hello," she said, suddenly very nervous.

She could see that the top of his head was covered in beads of sweat, even though it was nearly forty degrees outside.

"Funny thing, seeing you at Sam's house last night," he said.

"Yeah, we go way back, didn't she tell you?"

"Nope, never came up," he said.

"Well, I've got to get back now," Becca said, walking toward the driver's door.

Gideon put a massive hand on the door frame, holding it fast. His eyes looked her over like he was a predator, and in that moment, she knew.

"Try anything and I'll scream," she said.

"I'm sorry," he whispered. "But the dreams have stopped. It's time for the roots to be nourished."

In one smooth motion, he slammed her head through the window of her car with his free hand. Her scalp burned from the shards of glass that got embedded in her hair. She hit the ground with a thud and feebly tried to crawl away.

She never saw the yellow shoe that came down on the back of her skull.

35

When Becca didn't come back in an hour, they started to worry. When it had been two hours, Sam drove Trey around town looking for her. They never found her or her car, though they did find some blood and glass in the parking lot at Eaton's and assumed the worst.

Sam left Trey in the car while she ran inside to buy the materials again. Trey sat in the passenger seat in a panic. He tried not to think about seeing Becca up in a tree like Kevin, but he couldn't help it. It didn't matter what they did or what they thought, this so-called Fifth Signet was ahead of them every step of the way. And their list of allies didn't bring him any confidence, either. Even if they could trust the Tenches on the surface, they still worshipped the

Rootmother. What side would they take when it was their goddess on the other end?

Sam returned with bottles, rags, lighters, and a gas can. She didn't say anything, but handed the items to Trey and sped out of the parking lot, heading for Local Pump. Once there, she again got out silently and filled the can, handing it back to Trey when she was done. Minutes later, they were back inside her house, dumping beer down the sink, all without speaking.

"She's dead," he said at last.

"Not yet, she isn't," Sam said. "Maybe they plan to have two sacrifices tonight, or maybe that piece of shit Abner told them about the mayor and they changed targets. In any case, she's alive until tonight—so the plan is unchanged."

"That's easy for you to say," Trey said. "She's not your—"

"My what?" Sam asked. "My girlfriend? Are you two fucking? Were you fucking in my blankets on my floor?"

"What?! No!" Trey blurted out. "She's my friend, that's all."

"Guess what, Trey? After tonight, we are either all gonna be friends or all gonna be dead."

He nodded and went back to dumping beer.

By the time the sun was starting to set, they were ready with six Molotov cocktails ready to go. Nance pulled up in the squad car a quarter past six, and the pair loaded up in the back.

"Where's Becca?" she asked.

"Gone," Trey said sourly. "They took her sometime this afternoon."

"Fuck," Nancy said.

The sheriff stepped on the gas and drove down the block. Only took Trey a moment to realize that they weren't heading toward the Crown.

"What's going on?" he asked.

Beside him, Sam pulled out the gun and held it in her lap.

"If they took Becca, then that means their plan has changed. We need to check on Arthur, now!"

She blew through more than one stop sign before screeching to a halt in front of a large Georgian that stood across from the mill. The front door was ajar, and all of the lights were on.

"God dammit, no!" she shouted as she bolted from the car.

Trey and Sam quickly followed after her, though Trey wished he wasn't the only one without a gun. As they pushed past the front door, Trey immediately noticed the smell of blood and wet bark. His stomach sank. They rounded the corner into Arthur's front room and found him.

The mayor was sitting in a plush chair, his torso slumped to the left. His head and part of his spinal column were lying on the floor beside him. The walls were covered in archaic symbols written in his blood. One phrase was in English: She Knows What You Did.

Nancy fell to her knees and started crying, holding the severed head in her hands. Trey felt panic returning as he remembered what it was like to perceive the world for those few moments as his nervous system shut down. He stepped off to the corner and vomited behind the couch.

"We have to go, Nance," Sam said, putting a hand on her shoulder. "We have to stop this. Becca is still out there."

"Go!" Nancy shouted. "Leave me here. Just take the car and go!"

Sam pulled Trey by the arm back out to the squad car. This time they both sat in the front.

The squad car slowed to a halt in front of Ansel's mansion. The pair got out without closing the doors, grabbed their supplies, and crept down the hill toward the woods. It didn't take long for them to hear faint voices talking, and the whimpers of Becca White.

Sam squeezed Trey's shoulder and reminded him to be quiet. She pulled the revolver out as they got closer to the clearing. They split the Molotovs equally between the two of them, and each chose a tree to hide behind. Trey tried to block out the sounds of Becca crying and focus instead on the talking, but he found it impossible.

Leaning around the base of the tree, as low to the ground as he was able, he looked out at the Crown. Nearly a dozen hooded figures stood in the center of the stones. They wore cloaks that were either black or dark green, and each held a torch aloft. It was the most stereotypical cult shit he could think of. In the back, tied to one of the rocks, was Becca, naked and bleeding all over. Trey shivered as he thought of her smiling at him with his blood running down her face.

At least she's alive, he thought. *We haven't lost yet.*

"It's time," an old woman shouted. "It's time to nourish the roots. Khythk'uhn! We implore thee, Green Goddess, Rootmother, Time-Shattered Elder One! We are here to complete the cycle, as was ordained before time! We have come to finish the ritual so that you may awaken."

"Bring the son!" another man shouted.

The way he could see Sam tense told him that it was likely Clinton Abner, her boss, who had just spoken.

A cloaked figure knelt in front of Becca. The man took off his hood, revealing a bald head. Sam covered her mouth as she let out a faint yelp. Only then did Trey recognize the man as Gideon Nelson, the Gym Teacher who had visited her the night before.

Fuck fuck fuck, he thought.

"Finish the cycle!" Another voice shouted.

"Complete the cycle!" yelled another.

Trey knelt down and clicked the lighter. He couldn't afford to be a moment too slow, or Becca would die. He clicked it again and again but the damn thing wouldn't ignite. His glasses started to slide down the bridge of his nose.

"Come on, you piece of shit," he whispered.

"Trey!" Sam shouted, but it was too late.

Gideon was picking Trey up by the neck, even as the bald man's body began to change. His skin split open as pieces of bark pressed out from underneath. Bones that sounded like branches cracked and snapped as the man grew taller, his clothing shredding and falling away. His hands had become claws made of roots and sticks, claws that dug the flesh from Trey's throat. By the time his transformation was complete, even his eyes had popped from their sockets, replaced by two holes that wept sap. The only part of him that still seemed human was his teeth. Trey clawed at the bark-covered fingers, trying desperately to get loose.

Then he was flying through the air again, and he slammed into the stone nearest to Becca.

"Trey!" she shouted, though her voice was hoarse.

He was dazed, but this time he knew he wasn't dead. He stood up and saw the hooded members of The Fifth Signet moving closer to him.

"Your time has come, outsider," one hissed.

Trey remembered dying. His knees began to buckle, and he staggered backward against the stone. It was warm and slick with something akin to algae. He recoiled and pushed himself back upright. Gideon roared and stomped back into the clearing. The monster was nearly eight feet tall, and no longer shaped quite like the man it had been, but more like a beast that looked as if it would be as comfortable on all fours as it was standing upright.

"I've already died once!" Trey shouted as he moved in front of Becca. "And Khythk'uhn sent me back! What does that mean for your shitty little religion, eh? *She* wanted me back, I think it was to stop you!"

"Trey!" Sam shouted. "A torch! Get a torch!"

Then she threw one of the Molotov Cocktails, unlit as it was, at the Gideon-thing. The bottle smashed, covering the lower half of the creature in gas. She threw another, just as it turned toward her, batting the thing away with one hand, though that too caused it to be covered in fuel. Trey took advantage of the momentary distraction and wrestled a torch from the nearest cultist. He charged forward and tossed it up at the wettest part of Gideon's midsection. It immediately burst into flames.

The Gideon-thing roared in agony, stumbling around as it tried to bat out the flames. The cult members rushed to its aid, but they were batted aside like Trey had been. Finally, it staggered to the center of the stones, the heat of the flames so hot that Trey felt the skin on his hands blister when he covered his face. The monster fell to its knees, and the burning bark began to slough off, revealing the dying man underneath.

Sam walked into the middle of the Crown with her gun raised. Gideon the man looked at her one final time before she shot him through the head, tears streaming down her face. She joined Trey in untying Becca. Trey took off his shirt and put it on her. She sobbed in his arms while Sam kept the pistol trained on the cult members.

"What now?" the old woman called out.

"We stopped it," Trey said. "You've failed. You can fuck off for all I care."

Then the old woman laughed.

"You only stopped one cycle," she said. "They have been stopped before. One day, when the time is right, she shall awaken, as shall all of the Old Ones, and then time shall end. This meant nothing. But I ask you again, *outsider*, now what will you do, trapped here in her domain?"

Trey took the gun from Sam and pointed it at the woman talking. Then he moved it from one to the other across the cloaked figures.

"I think we're at a stalemate here," he said calmly. "You can try and kill me, but I might come back. I can try and kill you, but you might come back. Do either of us want to take that chance? I think you leave us be, and we will do the same to you."

"Very well," the woman said. "You were returned by the Rootmother. Perhaps it was for a purpose."

"One more thing," Trey said, before they all faded into the night. "Which one of you is Clinton Abner?"

The closest to him, whom he had wrestled the torch from, dropped his hood. Trey squeezed the trigger twice, causing the stones to reverberate with the twin explosions. He realized it had been much easier that time. The Principal dropped to his knees before falling onto his side.

"That was for Kevin and Chance," Trey said. "Now the rest of you get out of here."

The other cloaked figures faded back into the shadows of the trees. Trey and Sam carried Becca out of the Crown and back toward the car. Once they were out of the ring of stones, they heard a heavy grinding sound. They turned and saw the stones of the Elder One's Crown pulling together like fingers on a massive hand closing into a fist. Nearly as soon as they were all touching, they opened again, and Gideon and Clinton's bodies were gone.

They didn't look back again, even after they were driving away.

36

After they got back to Sam's house, they helped Becca get cleaned up, and they dressed her in some of Sam's clothes. The three of them huddled on the floor together in a singular embrace, none wishing to be separated from the others for that night at least. Though Trey was confident that his gambit with the cult would hold for tonight, he couldn't be so sure about the coming days.

As the hours ticked by, none of them spoke, but they didn't sleep either. Finally, it was Becca who talked first, her voice still hoarse from screaming in the woods.

"Thank you," was all she said.

They hugged her tighter, and the silence returned for a time.

"What are you gonna do?" Sam asked, finally.

"What do you mean?" Trey replied.

"Now that you're stuck here. What will you do?"

"I've given that some thought this evening, actually," he said with a wry smile. "First, I'm gonna put up a blog post and release a final episode for *The Dead and the Undead*, ending the show and dedicating it to Kevin. Then I'm gonna transfer what little money I have to the credit union here, make sure my friends and family know I'm not dead, see if the Best family will forgive me enough to sell me a house…"

"And then what?" Becca piped up. They could tell he was making them work for it.

"I'm going to start a new podcast, of course!" he chuckled. The women rolled their eyes at him like he was a child. "No, I'm serious. Tench said that there were other towns like this, and he made it sound like The Fifth Signet extended beyond Jackson Point. I want to create something that not only chronicles my experiences here, but can be a resource for others fighting this shit around the world."

"Jesus Christ you can be a pompous ass," Sam snickered.

"Maybe so, but I don't know what else to do with myself. Try and write that book, I guess."

"What will you call it?" Becca asked, cuddling

into him closer, her fingers brushing his chest and those of Sam.

"*Savage Stories*," he laughed. Both women glared. "I'm kidding. I was actually thinking, *Backwoods Grindhouse*."

"That's a little sensational, don't you think?" Becca asked.

"Sounds pretty white," Sam muttered.

"It needs to be over the top. That way, most people think it's an act, but the people who know will know. And then maybe we can get some help, combine what we know, and find a way to get out of here."

"I guess that makes sense," Becca yawned. "I'm sure we can convince you to change it in the morning."

A few minutes later, both women were asleep on the floor, and Trey joined them. Before he closed his eyes, he prayed for the first time in he didn't know how long—not to God, but to the Rootmother. Trey prayed that time would move forward, that he wouldn't have to relive this again.

In the morning, when Trey woke up, the first thing he did was look at his phone to see what the date was. All he could do was laugh.